The Christmas Spirit

Other Books by Alexandrea Weis

Realm
The Secret Brokers (Book 1)
Sisters of the Moon

By the Multi-Award-Winning Duo
Alexandrea Weis with Lucas Astor

The Magnus Blackwell Series
Blackwell: The Prequel (A Magnus Blackwell Novel, Book 1)
Damned (A Magnus Blackwell Novel, Book 2)
Bound (A Magnus Blackwell Novel, Book 3)
Seize (A Magnus Blackwell Novel, Book 4)

The St. Benedict Series
Death by the River (A St. Benedict Novel, Book 1)

Forthcoming by Alexandrea Weis

Have You Seen Me?
A Locket of Time

Forthcoming by Alexandrea Weis with Lucas Astor

The Chimera Effect
The Secret Salt Society
A River of Secrets (A St. Benedict Novel, Book 2)

The Christmas Spirit

ALEXANDREA WEIS

The Christmas Spirit

Cover design by Michael J. Canales
www.MJCImageWorks.com

ISBN: 978-1-64548-041-9

Published by Rosewind Romance
An imprint of Vesuvian Books
www.RosewindRomance.com

Printed in the United States

10 9 8 7 6 5 4 3 2 1

Chapter One

C louds, heavy with black rain, hung outside the high-rise office window, obliterating any chance of seeing the red and green holiday lights strung along the Cumberland River. The loss of the one highlight of her corner office added to Courtney Winston's dismal mood. She stared out, hungry for a hint of Christmas spirit, and wishing for a break from the inner numbness consuming her.

Courtney spun her chair around to her curved dark cherry desk and took in the office she'd received with her Director of Corporate Accounts promotion. The muted shades of gold and burgundy complemented the red leather furnishings. She'd purchased the framed pictures of Nashville's historic sites from a local gallery to enliven the space. But six months into her new position, the workspace remained as confining as all the others she'd occupied since coming to Harling and Wind Accounting Firm.

The stale, heated air pushing through the vents made the small bells tinkle on her plastic desktop tree.

She touched a silver ball with a pen and then frowned.

Is this going to get any easier?

Her office door flew open.

"Your literary agent has been trying to get you on your cell." Her stout, redheaded secretary approached her desk with raised brows. "She rang my phone and said you have to call her back right away."

Courtney gripped her pen and sat up, trying to appear busy. "Thanks, Bev."

"Are you coming to the office Christmas party tonight?" The bubbly clip in Bev's tone contrasted with the depressing atmosphere. "A lot of single guys from legal will be there."

Courtney checked her first reaction—to feign gagging—and put on a tolerant sneer. "I'd rather have my eyes gouged out with holly than let another man into my life."

Bev's shoulders drooped and her rosy cheeks sagged. "Come on. It's been a month already. You need to forget about him and get back on the horse."

Courtney held her breath and counted to five while squeezing her pen. If she didn't, she might start crying again or throw papers around her office. She considered her restraint a vast improvement. No matter how wretched she felt, or how much she wished to bury herself in bed, Courtney had to put on a stoic face for the office.

"I'm not interested in breaking in another man, or have them break me in." She held up her hand, wishing for better control of her sharp tongue. "That came out wrong. Forget I said it."

Bev leaned against the door, her eyes probing her boss.

"They're not all bad, you know? You just ended up with a rotten apple."

Courtney stood, tired of the conversation. "Yeah, well, I'm going to stay away from all apples for a while."

"At least come to the party and have a drink with me." Bev bounced on her toes. "It will be fun and my only night away from Ron and the kids."

"Sorry, can't." She hated herself for letting Bev down, but she had a great excuse. "I've got to pack tonight. I have to be on the road first thing in the morning."

"I envy you." Bev hugged herself, a dreamy look on her face. "A week on a fifty-acre farm in the mountains of Tennessee for the holidays—it's so romantic."

Courtney tossed the pen to her desk. "A week with my parents and my brother flaunting his new, perfect wife is far from romantic."

"I thought you liked Missy." Bev's cheerful grin buckled. "She's your best client, and it was your idea to introduce her to Matt."

"I do like her." Flashes of the pretty blonde with doe-brown eyes reduced her dreariness. "I admire how she's built her booming bakery shop. I even like the way she does her accounting. It's just hard being around her and my brother when they're so ... happy."

"Well, at least you won't be stuck in an apartment with your husband, two kids, your in-laws, and their dog with halitosis."

Courtney could always count on Bev to put a little perspective on things.

"What do all the Christmas cards say? *'It's the memories that matter'.*"

Bev rolled her eyes. "Probably written by men who've never had to taser someone to get the latest Xbox for their kid." She eased out of the office and shut the door.

Courtney took a deep breath and refocused. She needed to stay sharp with her agent. Jan Fletcher could be tough, but that she believed in Courtney's writing was everything.

She picked up her cell and found Jan's number.

After only one ring, she answered. "Girl, you owe me."

The ascorbic but optimistic tone stirred Courtney's floundering hope. Her heart sped up.

"They liked it?"

Jan sighed into the speaker. "They liked it."

Courtney wiggled in her chair, feeling more enthusiastic than she had in weeks.

"But they have a lot of changes," Jan said with a cautionary lilt.

She didn't like hearing that. "What kind of changes?"

"Rewrites—lots of them. They want to keep the love story but change the whole backstory on the hero and heroine. I'm emailing you what they want now. The bad news is, they need the entire book by the first."

Courtney grabbed her pen and hurried to scribble notes on her legal pad. "First of February is doable."

"First of January," Jan corrected.

An anchor sank to the bottom of Courtney's stomach. "What?"

"You heard me." Jan's voice turned colder. "That this big publisher wants your book is huge for you. They could put you in every bookstore across America and get you enough press to put you on the map. You could get out of that office and write full time, but you have to get the story up to speed before they give you a contract."

She'd not expected to spend her holidays working. Courtney cringed, picturing her mother's reaction to the news.

"I had plans to go to my parents' farm for the week to take a break before the year-end accounts are due."

"Do you want to be a writer or an accountant?"

The challenge in Jan's voice bothered her. Courtney loved her agent and signed with her to get this opportunity; she just hadn't expected to be faced with the ultimate decision so soon.

"To be one you're going to have to cut back on the other." Jan's tone softened. "You can't do both and be any good at either. We've talked about this. You committed to do whatever it takes for your writing."

Her breath hitched at the mention of her childhood dream—to be a writer. Creating stories was the hoped-for goal she'd kept hidden while pursuing an accounting degree in college. After words, numbers had been her second love and one of the few things she remembered sharing with her dad—counting sheep every night before she went to bed.

"What would you suggest I do?"

"Skip going to your parents' farm. Find a nice secluded cabin and spend Christmas there, revising your manuscript. You're going to need several days of quiet to get through all the work the publisher wants done."

The tight deadline added to the nervous flutter in her belly. "What if I can't do it? What would they do if I can't get all the changes done in time?"

"Don't even go there." Jan raised her voice. "You want this, then bust your butt. There's no second chance with this publisher."

Courtney wiped her brow, already breaking out in a cold sweat. Deadlines she could handle, but they had always been accounting ones. With her two previous novels, the small publisher who handled them had given her leeway because of her job. There would be none of that now.

She had climbed the ladder of success at her accounting firm and knew what it took to get ahead. However, the stress of being a writer didn't compare to the corporate world. She had no one to share her deadlines with—everything was all on her.

You can do this.

"Any idea where you'll go?"

Jan's voice interrupted the list of things Courtney ticked off in her head. She had a lot to arrange before getting out of town.

She turned to her computer, imbued with a steadfast resolve. "I don't even know where to look."

"Should be plenty of places outside of Nashville. There are tons of mountains there, right?" Jan paused and the sound of rustling papers came through the speaker. "Gotta be nicer than New York. The only close place we can go to escape is New Jersey."

Jan hung up, leaving Courtney to hunt for a getaway. With Christmas only days away, she knew finding a place would be a challenge. Unfortunately, explaining to her mother why she wasn't coming to the farm would be an even bigger nightmare.

Not attending one of Laurie Winston's holiday events was tantamount to calling for an open rebellion. You had to toe the line by donning ugly sweaters at the family Christmas Eve party and wear candy cane pajamas to bed. You had to greet Christmas morning with all the enthusiasm of a five-year-old. If you didn't share in Laurie's celebration, you became a second-class citizen and suffered an entire year of emails about your lack of cheer.

In her heart, Courtney knew this was for the best, even if the result ended up disappointing her mother. She had to make the effort. Jan was right—she was a writer in her heart, not an accountant.

She scoured the internet for cabins close to Nashville. Several search engines took her to sites with five-star accommodations and places that looked like they hadn't been lived in since Daniel Boone explored the area.

She went from glamping sites to places that promised rustic getaways, but everything that fit her timeframe and budget showed up as booked or had a waiting list.

Apprehension churned in her stomach. If she didn't find anything, what would she do? Camp out in her parents' barn with a *Do Not Disturb* sign on the doors.

Like my mother would ever pay attention to that.

She couldn't give up, not with everything on the line.

Courtney decided to expand her search area and check for cabins farther outside of Nashville. She didn't care how long she had to drive to get there and considered a greater distance from her parents' farm a good idea.

Please send me a Christmas miracle.

A throbbing headache popped up behind Courtney's eyes after

she'd stared at her monitor for over two hours. Her back ached for a break as she'd almost exhausted her search for a cabin. At this point, she would settle for anything with a roof and running water. Even though roughing it had never been her thing, she would suffer for the sake of her book.

Her office door eased open and Bev walked inside, carrying a mug of coffee.

"I noticed you skipped lunch. I figured you might need this." She strolled across the room and slid the cup onto her desk.

The reviving aroma of her favorite nutty mocha blend called to Courtney. She stretched out her back and closed her hands around the mug.

"You're a lifesaver."

Bev fanned her with a stack of pink paper. "You got a few messages as well."

Courtney lifted the cup and gave her secretary a guilty smile. "Sorry. I turned off my phone."

Bev put the messages on the desk. "Most are clients eager to get word on their quarterly returns. I got a call from Mr. Hardy, with Hardy Car Dealerships. He asked you to call him about his deductions for next year. Kent Weeks, with Weeks Car Wash, also wants to speak to you about his health insurance—"

Courtney raised a hand. "They can all wait until after the holidays. If anyone else calls, tell them I have already left for Christmas."

Her secretary angled her head around to get a look at Courtney's computer screen. "What are you doing that makes you want to avoid your clients?"

She set her coffee down. "I have to find a secluded cabin for Christmas." She slumped in her chair. "I've got a deadline for my new book with that publisher I told you about—the really big one. But they want a ton of changes by the first of the year. My agent suggested a quiet cabin in the woods over Christmas, so I can work." She waved at her computer screen. "The only problem is every cabin from here to Knoxville is booked."

Bev sat on one of the red leather chairs in front of her desk. "What about your parents' farm? Why can't you find a secluded spot there and work?"

"You know how my mother feels about working over the holidays—every decoration, Christmas cookie, and present is a big deal. She stuffs my itinerary with parties, has relatives I didn't know existed at the farm, and complains if I'm not perky. I'll never get anything done."

Bev winced. "Laurie will be devastated when you tell her you're not going."

Courtney stiffened at the thought of dealing with her mother. Her guilt had already eaten a hole in her stomach.

"I'll come up with an excuse."

"Just don't say anything to her until I go home for the day," Bev pleaded. "Your mother will only call and pester me to make you go to the farm. I want to be well out of firing range." Bev motioned to the monitor. "What have you come up with?"

Courtney pointed to a map with blue dots, showing hundreds of cabin locations on her computer. "Nothing yet. I've been looking anywhere within a decent drive of here, but everything is booked. I never realized so many people rent cabins for Christmas."

Bev scanned the screen. "Ron and I did that once, a few years ago, before the kids came along. We got away to a place outside of Gatlinburg. Ron wanted to avoid his mother and mine."

A hopeful Courtney put her hands on the keyboard. "You wouldn't happen to remember the name."

"How could I forget?" Bev chuckled. "It's called Stone Mountain Lodge."

Courtney arched an eyebrow. "Stone? That's your son's name."

Bev blushed and gave a curt nod. "Yep."

She typed in the name on her search engine and waited for the website to appear.

A picturesque log cabin surrounded by lush woods made of pine and oak trees popped up on the homepage. Courtney thought she'd combed through practically every camp site in Tennessee but didn't remember seeing this one. Intrigued, she went through the menu to discover more.

There was a photo of the main lodge with a description of the history. The palatial three-story building, built out of stone and timber, sat nestled next to a snowcapped mountain. The rugged terrain and sense of isolation appealed to her—the perfect place to get away.

Bev pointed to an address in the righthand corner of the screen. "It's secluded and pretty high up in the Smoky Mountains. There was lots of snow and scenic trails when we were there, but Ron and I didn't spend much time outdoors."

Courtney grinned as she studied the page. "Which would explain why your four-year-old son is named Stone."

"Yeah," Bev added. "That was a really good trip."

She clicked through pictures and descriptions of the log cabins they offered. They were all modest but roomy and built out of large timbers with lots of windows. She liked the rustic details and the spacious porches. The website boasted wide hearths with all the firewood a person could burn during their stay.

Bev settled back in her chair. "We rented one of the cabins close to the lodge. But I know they had some farther away and a lot more remote."

She clicked through a few more pictures of the mountains surrounding the cabins. Courtney could almost feel her creativity sparking to light at the idea of writing in such a locale.

"Remote is good. And it's only a four-hour drive from here."

Bev pointed to a yellow banner on the right of the homepage, flashing information on the cabins. "Yeah, but remote means no Wi-Fi or cable. You sure you're up for that?"

A tickle stirred in Courtney's belly. Something about the landscape and the location clicked with her.

"Sounds perfect. Now to see if they have any cabins left."

Courtney was about to type in her information when Bev stopped her.

"I'd call and see if they can take you. Ron builds these kinds of websites for his clients and he says half the time they're inaccurate about whether a place is booked or not. He always nags me to call to book our hotel rooms and stuff."

The ringing of a phone from Bev's office drifted into the room.

Her secretary stood and offered Courtney a sly grin.

11

"I bet if you tell them you're a soon-to-be-famous writer, they'd find a cabin for you. It worked for Stephen King, right?" Bev hurried out of her office.

After Bev shut the door, Courtney reread the headline on their website.

Secluded cabins set in the heart of the Smokies.
We guarantee nothing but peace and quiet.

For Courtney, getting away from her family and her job had never been a consideration. Writing was something she fit in after work or time with friends or family. Most of her writing occurred during the wee hours of the morning when she was assured no one would disturb her. This would be the first time she'd made writing a priority.

Confidence surged through her as Courtney dialed the number. She said a silent prayer that they would have an available cabin. If this didn't work, she might have to spend the holiday in a hotel where no one could find her.

"Stone Mountain Lodge."

The voice on the other end of the line was male, had a gravelly quality to it, and sounded decidedly cheerful.

"Ah, hi, my name is Courtney Winston and I'm looking to rent a cabin over the Christmas holiday. Something secluded. And I need it starting tomorrow."

She cringed, knowing she had rambled, but her nerves had gotten the better of her.

"Tomorrow, eh? Well, Ms. Winston, I do have one cabin

available. It's remote and we usually don't rent it out. There are some things you need to know about the place before—"

"I'll take it," she practically shouted into the phone.

"Just like that." The sunny quality in his tone dwindled. "You haven't heard about it. You might not like what I have to say."

Her grip tightened on her phone, letting her desperation seep into her voice. "I've been looking online and everyone is booked. If it's livable and not occupied by raccoons, I'll be fine. It's either your cabin or I'll be stuck coming up with a much more dismal alternative. Please. You're my last hope."

A few seconds of silence curled her toes.

"Well, that's a first," he said in a smoky murmur. "I've never been anyone's last hope before."

She liked the seductive quality in his voice. Pictures of what he might look like dashed across her mind. Tallish, muscular, brown hair, deep-set eyes—

Stop that. You don't need another mistake in your life.

"The fee is seventy-five a night for an unstocked cabin." He was back to business again. "One hundred a night for a stocked one."

"Stocked?" She nervously reached for her pen. "What do you mean?"

"With groceries. Most people bring their food, but we can stock cabins with the basics for an extra charge."

She liked that. No need to stop and pick up food along the way. "Stocked, definitely. One less thing to worry about."

"How many are staying in the cabin?"

"Just one. Me." She paused and then hurried to come up with

an excuse. "I have work to get done over the holidays and need peace and quiet."

"What do you do that has you working over the holidays?"

The distraction of his alluring voice faded, and a jittery sensation took over. Courtney didn't mind sharing that she wrote romance novels with friends, family, and coworkers, but the peculiar looks she'd gotten in the past from strangers made her wary.

"I'm an accountant in Nashville."

"And you want to come to the Smokies to get your work done?"

She settled back in her chair, enjoying the mystery she'd created in his mind. "I just need someplace without distractions to catch up."

Silence crowded the line and brought a lump to her throat. Had she said too much? Perhaps come across as a serial killer? The questions churned the acid in her stomach.

"Okay, if you want the cabin, it's yours." He had the same affable tone as when she'd first called. "Give me an email, and I will send you a link where you can download your info and give us a credit card to hold the reservation."

She pumped her fist into the air. "Thank you."

Courtney gave him her office email, making sure to spell out her first and last name so he would remember.

"There will be directions on the link on how to get here and what we offer," he said after taking down the information. "When you arrive, come to the lodge and ask for me, Peter Morris."

She even liked his name. "Thank you, Mr. Morris."

"Call me Peter. Everyone does."

He hung up and she stared at her phone.

With my luck, he's probably married.

The ping of an incoming email caught her attention.

Dear Ms. Winston,

It was wonderful speaking to you.
Here is the link.
reservations@stonemountainlodge.com
Looking forward to seeing you tomorrow. Have a

pleasant drive up.

Peter

"That was fast."

Courtney went to the site and filled out the necessary information. Once done, she hit the confirm reservation button and waited.

When the reservation went through, she breathed a sigh of relief. She had a cabin, and an excuse to get away from her family. Things were looking up.

Courtney sent off a quick text to Jan.

> Got my cabin in the woods. Will have
> something for you after I get back.

She was about to set her phone aside when Jan texted back.

> Call if you need me. Make this work,
> and you'll be on your way.

Courtney read the text twice, excited for the change a successful book would bring. Then dread shadowed her enthusiasm—her mother would be heartbroken.

Christmas had been a big event ever since her mother married Gerald Winston. Courtney's stepfather had indulged her mother's attempt to make each Christmas celebration grander than the last. Only one Christmas in Courtney's memory had been very sedate. She was five years old when she spent the last Christmas with her dad before he left. Courtney believed her mother's frenzied celebrations were meant to make up for his absence, and she'd enjoyed all the over-the-top festivities, but this year, she felt some time away from her mother would be a good thing.

But how are you going to convince Mom of that?

Chapter Two

Bitter cold deepened its grasp on her exposed face and hands. The heater was little help as her small car trekked slowly up the mountain pass. Piles of snow, mixed with dirt and leaves, covered each side of the narrow road, marking where the snowplows had done their job. But there was still lots more of the fluffy stuff atop the tall trees, brush, and the occasional sign along the side of the country road. For anyone else, the picturesque mountain pass, its snowy banks twinkling in the afternoon sunlight, would have been idyllic for the Christmas season. For Courtney, it was a huge pain in the butt.

She tightened her grip on the steering wheel as the car shimmied on the slick road. The escape to the mountains better be worth the expense, aggravation, and hypothermia she'd already endured. If this didn't give her the inspiration and quiet she needed for her writing, she would never let Bev hear the end of it.

Then there was the guilt her mother piled on after hearing the news. The harsh words they exchanged had been eating at her since leaving Nashville.

"You're going to the mountains to write a book at *Christmas?*"

Her mother shouted into the phone as Courtney packed her

car.

"I have to go. This is my chance, Mom. If I don't get these edits done, the publisher will pass on my book."

"But what about Christmas?" Her mother sounded brittle. "We've always been together. And this is the first year with your brother's new wife. What will Missy think if you're not here?"

The reminder of Matt's happiness only amplified her desire to run away. "You have Missy to stand in for me at the party. No one will notice when I'm not there."

"I'll notice," her mother loudly protested. "Is this about him? Are you running away to forget about what he did to you?"

Courtney hated the way her mother could read her like a book. Did nine months of lodging give her mother psychic abilities, or was it all those years of snooping around her bedroom? The question often kept Courtney up at night.

"This is about me and what I want in life. I want to pursue my writing. You know what my stories mean to me."

"And your family means nothing. Is that what you're saying?"

"You know that's not it." Courtney reined in her emotions—she would never win with her mother. "I have to go. It's a long drive."

Her mother's voice, seething with all the disappointment Laurie Winston could muster, haunted her during the drive. Their argument made her glad for the escape, but also worried about how she could ever make it up to her mother. Laurie had been her biggest fan and the one who encouraged her to write for as long as she could remember.

Courtney guessed this was the price all writers paid for their art—missed holidays and turbulent family emotions. In the end, she prayed the trip would be worth it. Then, she could make her mother proud.

A line of trees alongside the road, blanketed in the freshly fallen snow, brought back memories of one Christmas and the snowball fight with her brother that had gone down in the record books. She remembered the way Gerald joined in on the fun, pelting her and Matt with snowballs. Her mother's obsession with the holidays paled in comparison to her stepfather's childlike exuberance for adventure. The two were well-suited for each other, and her stepfather had almost filled the hole left by her dad's departure. Gerald's deep bellow rang in her ears, making Courtney itch to turn her car around and head for the farm.

A sloping rooftop, covered with glowing cedar shingles, broke through a cluster of pines, silencing her longing. Between gaps in the trees, the three-story lodge appeared. Built from thick wood logs and stone, it sat perched on a peak overlooking a snow-packed valley. The retreat's walls of windows glowed with warm yellow light against the late afternoon sky.

Courtney careened her car around a bend in the narrow road, and then the full majesty of the rustic home came to light. Stone steps climbed to an arched portico big enough to drive a car through. The front door, made of the same cedar as the exterior, had a latticework and glass transom, and long windows on either side. One stone chimney rose to the third floor. Two other chimneys poked out from the rear, while two short balconies jutted from the upper floors. The building was a perfect complement to the rich woods surrounding it. Stone Mountain Lodge surpassed

Courtney's expectations.

She pulled up to a line of large boulders at the lodge's entrance. A fresh dusting of snow covered the three other cars parked there. One was a Jeep equipped with off-road tires. She admired the rugged vehicle, picturing it tearing through trails across the inhospitable landscape, far away from people.

Courtney climbed from her car, still caught up in her daydream of living a quiet life in the mountains when the bitter wind hit her face. She hugged her blazer closer, wishing she had worn something more than her favorite tweed.

The gentle thud of a door closing made her spin around.

A man—tall, lean, and moving in an assertive stride—came from the entrance to the lodge. He walked down the stone steps, flashing a friendly smile while his piercing blue eyes zeroed in on her. His square jaw, shadowed with stubble, and his sharply carved cheekbones awakened a tingle in her belly. The crunch of his boots on the snow as he approached raised her heart rate. The closer he got, the better looking he became.

"Ms. Winston?" he said in the same gravelly voice she'd fantasized about on the phone.

Courtney raised her head, remembering to smile. "Are you Mr. Morris?"

He extended his hand, the bulk beneath his brown leather jacket hinted at a man who liked to keep in shape.

"Peter, remember? Welcome to the Stone Mountain Lodge."

She struggled to remove one of her gloves and then dropped it on the ground.

Before she could bend over, he retrieved it.

"I'm Courtney," she said, taking the glove from him.

His energetic handshake surprised her. He had an upbeat manner, the kind that permeated the air and made everyone happier for being around him. But his vivaciousness didn't rub off on her. Anyone acting chipper instantly aroused her suspicion.

Peter dropped his hand and stood before her, studying her face. Courtney's mind raced with clever comments, but her mouth was sluggish, her tongue twisted. A knot of awkwardness sprouted in her chest, but still, she was unable to tear her gaze away from him.

Peter broke the spell and motioned to her car. "I'd hoped you'd bring someone with you."

A hint of disapproval crept into his voice—or maybe it was her, overreacting again. Ever since her breakup, she'd been hypersensitive about her interactions with men. The snide comments and cutting remarks that had filtered into her doomed relationship remained fresh in her mind. She'd become so attuned to his dissatisfaction that she'd heard a dissenting tone in every conversation since the day he walked out. The tension their relationship had created, the self-doubt and dejection, came roaring back.

"Is there a problem?" she asked in a snippy voice.

"No. Not at all." He held his hands up. "Just don't understand why you want to be all alone to do work in a cabin in the woods during Christmas." Peter went around to the rear of her car. "All sounds very mysterious."

Courtney hesitated, nervous about telling him of her real intentions.

"Isn't a remote cabin in the woods a perfect place to get away and get things done? Why else would you have one?"

He opened the hatch on her car. "The first owner would agree with you. He built the cabin where you're going to stay after the lodge was completed." He lifted her two overnight bags and set them on the ground. "No one ever tore the place down because there always seems to be someone looking for a hideaway in the woods."

He was about to reach for her computer case when she stepped up and grabbed it.

"I'll take that." She hugged the case to her chest.

He eyed the case with an arched brow. "There won't be any internet service in your cabin. That computer won't work if you have to download figures or anything to your company."

"Yes, I remember you saying that." She gave him a guilty smile.

"And your cell services will be spotty. For some reason, that cabin has lousy reception."

That awakened a twinge of alarm. "Just my cabin. That's weird, but maybe also a good thing. I'll need to avoid distractions while working on my book."

His brow creased, hiding the blue in his eyes. "Your book? Are you a writer?"

"Yes, I've got a big deadline to make. It's the reason I'm here."

His face darkened. "But when you called to book the cabin, you said you were an accountant."

How many people never hear anything they were told? But he remembered their conversation.

She lowered the computer case. "I'm an accountant, but I have a side gig as a writer. I sometimes wonder if I should give up writing and concentrate on my career at the firm where I work."

"A person should never give up what's in their heart. It's who they are." He picked up her bags. "But I understand. My mother is still waiting for me to finish my master's in education."

"Why haven't you?"

He stopped and browsed the snow-topped trees dipping down the side of the mountain, and the tall walls of the lodge. "And give up all this?" His smile lifted the corners of his eyes, crinkling the edges. "Never."

The tingle in her belly intensified. Then a heavy, dull throb started in her chest and radiated out to her limbs, making the bag in her arms unbearably heavy. That was what he had left her with—uncertainty. She questioned herself more and more since the breakup. The decisive woman she'd treasured had vanished.

Peter's intrusive gaze was on her, sizing her up as if he anticipated a reply.

She dropped her head and fiddled with the zipper on her computer case. "Do you need me to sign the register or something?"

"No, I got everything you sent me online." He nodded to the off-road Jeep. "We'll take this to your cabin. Your car won't get through the road, especially with all the new snow we got today."

She looked around at the trees surrounding them. "How far is the cabin?"

He nodded at the woods to the right of the lodge. "About two miles that way but might as well be ten in this weather."

She stared into the trees, mesmerized by the way the wind rocked their tops, sending snow to the ground. A funny twinge erupted in her chest. Trepidation brought a frown to her lips.

Are you sure about this?

The *thunk* of her bags loaded into the Jeep carried around her.

"Are you going to be okay alone up there?" Peter was at her side. "Maybe you should stay at the lodge. Some guests will be clearing out by Christmas Eve. I could arrange for you to have one of our suites."

Her chin jutted out, fueled by her obstinacy. "Why? You don't believe I can handle it?"

He went to the passenger side of his Jeep and opened the door, keeping up his winning smile.

"I don't believe anything of the kind. All I know is sometimes people think they want to be alone when what they need is a friend."

The fading afternoon light caught in his eyes and for a moment, she considered his offer. Then the weight of the computer case reminded her of her book.

"Thanks, but what I need is to be somewhere with little chance of interruptions."

She struggled as she climbed into the Jeep, ignoring Peter's extended hand.

Courtney finally got settled in her seat and caught her breath.

Peter chuckled and tipped his head to her. "If you say so."

She enjoyed his confident stride as he went around the Jeep, the way he carried his broad shoulders, and the ropelike muscles poking over the collar of his leather jacket. Peter exuded a calm reassurance she'd never felt from a man. He didn't seem the type to play games or hide secrets. Nor did he come across as full of himself or difficult to deal with like Kyle.

Her former lover and client had been full of bluster and stormed into conference rooms like an angry hurricane. He'd intimidated everyone at the accounting firm, including her. The day he'd asked her to dinner, she'd been too afraid to turn him down.

Peter is too good for you. Forget about him.

Her inner voice sounded as defeated as the day Kyle told her their relationship was over.

"What kind of writer are you?"

His smoky voice lifted her from her doldrums as he settled into the driver's seat.

"Ah …" She had to think for a minute. "I write novels. Fiction novels."

He put his key in the ignition. "What do you write about?"

She gripped the computer bag, summoning her courage. "Love stories. Contemporary romances."

The throaty engine roared, blotting out the *whoosh* of the wind around them.

"Do you write under your name or a pen name?"

The pungent aroma of gasoline and oil curled her nose.

She turned to him, attempting to hold her breath. "Why? Are you going to check me out?"

He put his hand on the stick shift. "Might just."

She noticed his wide palms and thick fingers. He had outdoor hands, not city hands like her ex.

"Well, then. I write under my real name." Courtney raised her gaze to the lodge. "Feel free to purchase my two other books. I could use the three dollars in royalties to cover the cost of this trip."

He chuckled. "I can see why you haven't given up your day job yet." Peter put the shifter into reverse and the abrasive grind of gears filled the air. "What's your new book about?"

Courtney clutched the computer bag. "A woman from Nashville finding love in an unexpected place."

She watched his profile, gauging his reaction as the Jeep backed away from the line of boulders.

Peter hit the brake. "Is it any good?"

"Should be by the time I leave here."

He pushed the stick shift into first gear. "Then you haven't got the story right where you want it yet."

She glared at him. "Hence the reason for the secluded cabin."

The Jeep lurched ahead. She gripped the door while still clutching her laptop, wishing there was another way to get to her cabin.

"I've heard about writer's block." Peter maneuvered the vehicle across the narrow road, heading toward a swath of tall pines. "They say the greatest writers suffered from it."

Her irritation briefly surpassed her fear of continuing her ride in his Jeep.

"I don't have writer's block. I have a publisher who wants me to make changes to the book before the first of the year."

The trees drew closer, and her eyes got bigger as she questioned if he planned to go through them. There was no path and no opening.

"Do you want to make these changes?"

She didn't look at him, but kept her sights on the trees, wondering if he had purposefully planned to frighten her by driving into them.

"I do if I want to get my book published."

"Why couldn't you make these changes back in Nashville?"

His inviting voice sent an unsettling tickle along her back and distracted Courtney from the narrow opening.

"Because I needed to get away," she croaked as a rising alarm cinched her throat. "Somewhere where I wouldn't be interrupted."

"Interrupted by whom? Your boyfriend?"

The question instantly erased her unease. She let go of the door and faced him, curbing her anger.

"If you must know, I recently ended a relationship. I thought we were good for each other; he thought he needed to see other people."

"Ouch." Peter winced. "We've all been there. Well, not me personally, but I get it."

She glowered at him, irritated.

He recoiled from her gaze. "I'm just saying, if he was stupid enough not to appreciate you, then he's not worth a second thought. No one is. If someone can't build you up, then run away. That's what my father always told me."

She loosened her grip on her laptop bag and faced him. "And how many women have you let go of?"

"What makes you think they were women?" He winked at her.

Courtney flopped back in her seat, dumbfounded. She was a pretty good judge of character, and the looks he'd given her, the hint of attraction had been unmistakable. Or perhaps she was worse at sizing up men than she'd believed.

"I'm sorry. I didn't think."

His musical chuckle surprised her. It wasn't deep like his voice, but soft and uplifting.

"I'm not gay, but you needed to lighten up. And to answer your question, I never let go of any woman. It's more like they let go of me."

She held back a snicker. *I know how you feel.*

Branches slapped the windshield as the car drove through the clump of trees. Courtney gulped, anxious for whatever waited for them behind the thick swath of leaves.

"Who was he?" he asked, raising his voice over the crush of twigs.

She reached for the handle to the right of her head, steadying herself as the car rocked. "Someone I knew from work. I helped set up the accounting program for his business."

The branches parted and a muddy road appeared. With round boulders on either side and tree branches hanging low over the path, the thoroughfare didn't appear wide enough to accommodate the Jeep.

The nauseating smell of gasoline and the bouncing of the car had her aching to roll down the window, but she feared getting stabbed by a branch.

"Is he the reason you want to be alone?"

"Not completely," she admitted with a sigh. "But I wouldn't be good with people right now anyway."

"I don't believe that. Don't become sadder by shutting

yourself away. All you do is deepen your pain."

No longer interested in the scenery, she turned to him.

"Living up here, you're just as cut off as I'll be in my cabin."

His grin added a mischievous glint to his eyes. "Ah, but at the lodge we have Wi-Fi. I'm not cut off from anyone. The only thing you'll have at the cabin is a landline connected to the lodge and unreliable cell service." He paused, keeping his gaze on her. "Still want to be alone?"

She faced the path ahead, her determination deepening. "More than ever."

Chapter Three

 he narrow path brought on a wave of nausea. A smidgen of
regret coursed through her. Maybe running away to write had
been an unrealistic plan, but then, to Courtney's relief, the path
widened. A clearing bordered by large rocks, caught in the last rays
of the evening sun that cast an eerie indigo glow all around the
Jeep. Behind the clearing, nestled between two tall spruce trees,
appeared a traditional, single-story log cabin.

The walls had thick beams stacked horizontally. Notched
edges at the corners jutted out, still showing the marks where the
ax had cleaved into the wood. The porch, supported by thick
knotted posts, had a graceful wood railing and stone steps that
matched the chimney rising from the side. Windows framed in the
same rugged wood sat on either side of the front door. There were
no garden beds, no potted plants, nothing to add a hint of
hominess. There was something cold and unwelcoming about the
place.

They parked in front of the porch and a face or figure appeared
carved into the front door. Courtney could not make out the
image, but the odd impression added to the unsettling tickle
climbing her spine.

"Some place, huh?" Peter turned off the engine. "It was built in 1888."

She thought of something he would like to hear. "It's beautiful."

Peter opened his door. "I'll help you get settled in."

She climbed from the car while Peter went to the rear of the Jeep. Courtney ventured closer to the cabin, eager to get a better look.

The shadows of the porch kept the subject on the door hidden at first, but as she eased into the shade, she caught a glimpse of the intricate carving.

A woman in a flowing robe had a raised hand, beckoning weary travelers to enter the cabin. Long, wavy hair cascaded around her shoulders and fanned out as if caught in a ghostly breeze. Her heart-shaped face, small chin, luminous, round eyes, and small nose gave her an angelic quality, but her smile came across as sinister.

The menacing portrait amplified the disconcerting vibe the house exuded. The unwelcoming figure almost made Courtney turn around and head back to the Jeep.

"Who is that?" She pointed at the door.

Peter came up to her with her bags tossed over his shoulder. "That's Perchta. She was a witch in Austria, where my family came from. She hands out rewards and punishments during the twelve days of Christmas. Although, the stories I heard growing up were more about her torturous punishments. She wasn't a very nice lady. I think there's a book on her in the cabin somewhere if you're interested."

Courtney went to the stone steps, mesmerized. "Someone wanted to carve a witch on the door? That's creepy."

His footfalls followed her up the steps and she turned to him.

"She grows on you after a while," he said, easing a key from his pocket.

Peter pushed the door open, and a loud groan echoed across the porch.

The musty aroma of the cabin permeated the fresh, crisp air.

Courtney wrinkled her nose and stepped backward.

"Sorry." Peter glanced at her. "The place hasn't been aired in a few weeks, but the smell dissipates quickly once you open the windows."

He slipped inside. Courtney went to follow him, but as she was about to cross the threshold, a funny sensation gripped her. Like becoming trapped in a vacuum—unable to move forward or turn back—she stood frozen, perched over the doorway.

"You okay?"

Peter's voice broke the spell.

She glanced around the porch, undone. "I'm fine. Just tired from the drive."

Peter reached across the wall next to the door. "I'll show you around and then let you get to work."

The last thing she wanted was for him to rush off and leave her alone in the spooky cabin. She peered into the darkened room, searching for something or someone. They weren't alone.

Stop it. You're exaggerating.

A flash of light from a three-tiered, deer antler chandelier above made her hands tremble. She chastised herself for acting skittish, but that icky sensation of someone watching her remained. Courtney focused on the rich cedar color of the log walls and shiny hardwood floors. A small living room had a cream sofa stuffed with red throw pillows and a cozy handmade quilt. An oval coffee table, made of rough wood, and an assortment of faded framed photographs finished off the room's decor. The stone mantel commanded her attention and the arch-shaped hearth beneath had a grate already stacked with logs.

The unpleasant smell dissipated as a nippy breeze from the open door swept across the room.

Peter set her bags on the sofa. "Let me get a fire going. Looks a lot homier with a fire."

She didn't believe him but held her tongue. Courtney set her laptop case on the coffee table and went to inspect a few of the old photos.

"Who are these people?"

He collected a box of matches from the mantel. "My family. We've owned this place for over a hundred years. I figured our old photos would make for interesting decorations."

She turned to him, impressed. "I thought you were a caretaker or manager. I never suspected you owned all this."

He struck a match, grinning. "Never judge a book by its cover, Courtney."

She chuckled and tucked a loose lock of hair behind her ear. "Touché."

Peter knelt and set the match to the kindling. He blew on the small flame, encouraging the fire.

While the fire grew, she got a closer look at the black and white pictures close to the front door. Most were of women in formal dresses with bustles and flowery hats. The men had long coats, vests, and top hats. The subjects' faces were somber and their poses unnatural.

We've come a long way with our selfies.

Most were taken in front of the lodge. The building appeared the same. There were a few more photos of the mountain and the woods, but not one of the pictures contained her cabin.

A sharp, refreshing green scent caught her attention. After the musty reek in the cabin, she welcomed the change. Courtney peeked around a short wall at the entrance, hunting for the source.

In a dining area corner, next to a square roughly cut table, stood a fir tree in a red stand. A scenic window along the far wall let in the late afternoon sun, and tapering fingers of light warmed the tree's branches.

"There's a Christmas tree in here."

Courtney slipped into the room. On the dining table were two yellow boxes. She approached them, teeming with curiosity.

"Yeah, we put trees and ornaments in all our cabins during the holidays." Peter's raised voice drifted in from the living room.

She lifted the top on the first box and found dozens of silver balls nestled in a silver garland. The shiny glass ornaments winked in the fading sunlight.

She lifted one of the balls, amazed at how fragile it was.

"Not something I expected."

"Glad you like it."

She spun around and caught him leaning against the wall at the entrance, smiling at her.

"Garland and decorations are in one box." He motioned to the box close to her. "Lights are in the other."

She set the ball back in the box, the heat rising on her cheeks. "Seems like a waste of time to decorate a tree just for me."

He frowned. "Where's your Christmas spirit?"

"I'm not big on Christmas."

"That's a shame." He walked past her to the kitchen. "I always like to think of this time of year as a reminder of all we should be grateful for."

"My mother would agree with you." She inspected the kitchen cabinets stained to match the walls. "She lives for Christmas. Every year she makes such a fuss."

"But you're avoiding that this year."

She went around him to a stainless compact refrigerator and opened the door.

"Your cabin comes fully stocked for one week," Peter said behind her. "Eggs, milk, a fresh fruit and cheese tray, a few vegetables, as well as some sliced deli meats." He pointed to the freezer on top. "Ice cream, two rib eyes, two pounds of ground meat, a few fillets of rainbow trout, and one chicken are in there."

He maneuvered around her, brushing up against her as he went to a small door next to the fridge.

"This is the pantry." He opened the door. "You have coffee, flour, sugar, a selection of canned soups, dried goods, and on the floor several cans of soda as well as bottled water."

She ran her fingers along the black tile countertops while checking the brand of coffeemaker.

"You've thought of everything."

She peered out the arched window over the sink. The trees behind the house appeared thicker than in front and had a trail breaking between two tall pines. She squinted at the snowy path, swearing she could make out the slightest impression of boot prints.

Peter slipped through an open door at the back of the kitchen. "Laundry room is through here."

The swath of light from a single bulb cast long shadows along the walls. A stackable washer dryer, coat rack, and large sink took up most of the space.

She eased up to the doorway as Peter went to a back door.

He patted the door. "Keep this and the front door locked at night. If you hear anything outside or get frightened …"

Peter eased past her and went to a white telephone attached to the kitchen wall by the fridge. "Pick up this phone. It's preprogrammed to dial direct to my cell. There's another at your bedside."

A chill went through her. "But I can still go outside on the porch and make calls, right?"

He shrugged. "Sometimes the reception works. Sometimes not so much. It's one of the quirks I wanted to tell you about this cabin, but you seemed desperate."

A knot twisted in her stomach. "What other quirks do I need to know about?"

"Nothing serious. People who stay here report having trouble with the appliances and electronic equipment. My electrician can't figure out the problem but thinks the location on the mountain may be the culprit. This place gets struck by lightning quite a bit in the spring." He picked up the receiver. "So, if you need anything, call and I will bring it out to you. If anything breaks, call and I will come and fix it. If anything happens, call and I will come and get you."

Her chill became an ice storm. "What could happen?"

He cocked one eyebrow. "In case anything does, I keep my phone on me twenty-four-seven."

She wrung her hands. "Good to know."

Peter motioned to a hallway on his left. "The bedroom is this way."

Peter collected her bags from the sofa and then showed her down a narrow hallway. Their footfalls elicited groans and creaks, but the rest of the house remained silent.

Along the wall made of thick logs were framed colored photographs that sharply contrasted with the ones in the living room. These were aerial shots of the forest backed by the snowcapped mountains. The pictures captured the beauty of the wilderness.

"These are stunning," she said while admiring an overhead view of her cabin.

Peter stopped and glanced at the photo. "I took that last summer with my new drone when I was doing photos for the insurance company." He browsed the wall. "These were the best ones. I learned taking pictures with a drone can be quite challenging."

Courtney sized up his profile. "In what way?"

"Because most of the pictures you take come out as a big blur."

She turned to the opposite wall, where windows overlooked a

sloping line of trees. Tingles rose along her arms, and the hair on the back of her neck stood. Someone kept an eye on her from the forest. The darkening sky accentuated her uneasy feeling.

This place will be even creepier at night.

A flash of lights came from the bedroom and urged her to hurry and join Peter.

She crossed beneath a rough-beamed doorframe and became instantly entranced by a rustic log, king-sized bed. It had lots of oversized pillows and a red and white quilt that she could imagine snuggling under during cold mornings. A painting of a peaceful sunrise painted in vibrant hues, crimsons and scarlets, complemented a chunky Southwest rug with a red, black, and ivory arrow-inspired pattern.

Peter set her bags on the bed. He flipped on a brass lamp on top of the unfinished log nightstand.

Courtney went to an unfinished six-drawer log dresser at the foot of the bed and opened one of the drawers. The aroma of cedar chased away the staleness left in the room. When she stood, she caught her reflection in the mirror mounted above the dresser.

She cringed at her disheveled dark brown hair and smeared pink lipstick. The circles under her tired brown eyes did little to bolster her confidence.

She hastily ran her hand through her thick hair while keeping a wary gaze on Peter as he walked across the room.

"A full bath is through there." Peter stopped and pointed at an ajar door. "There's plenty of hot water and a heater in the bathroom. Extra towels and blankets are in the cupboard next to the bedroom door. If you need more blankets or towels, call me.

In case you lose power, which can happen, I have lanterns on a table by the front door, and in your bedroom. If the power goes out for longer than a few hours, I'll come and take you to the lodge. We have a generator there. For anything else—"

She pointed to the phone. "Call you."

He rubbed his hand across his chin. "Some people aren't into being cut off from the world. They want to know there's always someone available."

Courtney liked the way his gaze stayed on her, but the scars left by her ex ran deep. Before Kyle, she would have enjoyed Peter's concern. There were days she questioned if she would ever recover from him.

"So, I'm to call if I see a bear or slice open an artery while chopping wood or something."

Peter went to a pair of thick red curtains, spanning the entire wall on the other side of the room. He shoved the heavy drapes aside, letting in the dying light.

A long window, overlooking the side of the cabin, gave a breathtaking view of the woods.

"A stack of firewood for the coming week is around the side of the house." He motioned to a pile of logs resting against the home directly under the window. "And as far as the bears go, they're sleeping."

"You've covered every contingency short of a nuclear disaster."

His slight smile lifted the energy in the room. "If that happens, we have a fallout shelter under the lodge. A great uncle's addition."

Peter's penetrating gaze darn near dropped her to her knees.

"On Christmas Day, I have dinner at the lodge for my family

and guests. Why don't I come by and pick you up? You could join us. We have a great feast."

She didn't know what scared her more, having dinner with his family or him. "No. Thank you, but I couldn't possibly."

"I'd feel better knowing you were with us at Christmas. No one should be alone on such a day."

She folded her arms, intrigued. "Do you ever take no for an answer?"

Peter raised one side of his mouth in a slight smirk. "I'll come by on Christmas morning and help you decide then." He headed back into the hallway. "My mother makes the best buttermilk biscuits in the world. An old family recipe. Would be a shame for you to miss them."

Courtney followed him into the living room. The heat from the roaring fire chased away the chill the cabin gave her. The warm golden glow made the strange pictures in the room eerily cozy.

The lights in the three-tiered, deer antler chandelier flickered.

Courtney glanced up and shuddered.

"Are you sure about staying here alone?" he asked, his reservations deepening his voice.

She took one last turn of the living room, caught the lights from the dining area, and hugged herself. She would make this work, no matter how unsettling. Her future depended on it.

"I appreciate your concern, Peter, but you don't have to worry about me. I'm tougher than I look."

He shook his head and opened the heavy front door. "I have a strange feeling all I will do until Christmas Day is worry about you." He leveled his steely blue eyes on her. "Call if you need me."

He pulled the door closed behind him.

She listened to his footfalls on the porch. Courtney went to the window as Peter hurried down the steps to his Jeep. She already missed his company.

But you barely know the guy.

The vibrations of the engine rumbled throughout the cabin. The beams from his headlights shone through the living room window, making her shade her eyes.

The tug of her apprehension got stronger as Peter turned the Jeep around in the clearing. There was an incomprehensible urge to run after him, but Courtney squashed the butterflies in her belly. She defiantly raised her head as his high-riding Jeep headed back toward the muddy trail.

The engine's throaty chug faded, and when the last echo disappeared, there was silence.

Except for the gentle swish of limbs against the cabin's roof, the stillness was new for Courtney. In the city, there was always the comfort of garbage trucks, traffic, street vendors, and noisy neighbors to let you know you were never alone. She couldn't remember a time when she'd felt so isolated. Even on the family farm, there had always been someone around.

Then that disturbing chill returned. She rubbed her arms and inched closer to the fire, hoping it was just the approaching night. The nagging sensation never went away, no matter how close she got to the flames.

Maybe this wasn't such a good idea.

The resolve she'd fallen back on numerous times kicked in. She'd come to the cabin to accomplish one goal—to rewrite her book.

It's time to get to work.

Courtney removed her laptop from her computer bag, comforted by the weight of the machine. She hugged it to her chest and walked toward the dining area, taking in the way the gazes in the old photographs followed her across the room.

The floor moaned when she arrived at the dining table. She pushed the boxes of decorations to the side. Before setting her laptop down, she stroked the smooth, unfinished wood, admiring its imperfections.

A swell of pride rose. She had done the unexpected, shocking herself and her family by getting away. She had always been mindful of others, giving in to the pressures placed on her by clients, old boyfriends, and her mother. She'd never defied what everyone else wanted and fit writing in when she could. Now, she was putting herself and her dreams first.

Courtney pulled up the copy of her book with all the notes from the publisher Jan e-mailed her. The red marks seemed to go on and on as she flipped through pages. The suggestions from the editor about character arcs, descriptions, and even the setting were a lot more than she'd expected.

No wonder Jan wanted me alone in the woods.

The more she read, the less she liked the comments. What the publisher wanted seemed bland and formulaic. She had a sinking feeling the tale about a Nashville accountant who finds love with a client—loosely based on her failed relationship—would end up like every other office romance ever written. Even if she did stick with the publisher's notes, she doubted she could get everything done in time. The complete rewrite would strip away the uniqueness of the characters, change the timeline of the story, and take out the things that she loved but the publisher didn't.

Courtney stared at the blinking cursor, not sure what to do. Her enthusiasm for her days of peace in the woods waned.

Perhaps changing her book was a mistake, but Jan had worked hard to get her the publishing deal. Should she sacrifice this story and sell out for a chance at fame?

Her confidence in her novel took a nosedive. She debated packing her stuff and calling Peter to come and get her.

"Every work of genius begins as a disaster," her stepfather once said.

She placed her fingers on the keys, deciding to listen to her publisher and agent. They knew best, right?

You got this.

Chapter Four

Night seeped through the dining room window, and a chilly draft hovered over the table by the time Courtney looked up from her laptop. She blinked at the change in light and then rubbed her arms. She'd lost all track of time. Her stomach rumbled and her back longed for a soothing stretch. Despite her aches, she was satisfied with what she'd accomplished. Confidence had replaced her doubt. She would get the story where the publisher wanted it before her deadline.

Her enthusiasm warranted a celebration, or at least someone to share the news with.

She dug her phone from her purse and checked her bars—barely one registered.

Courtney walked around the house, raising and lowering her phone, checking her coverage. She was at the front door, about to step outside when a surge in her bars gave her some hope.

She froze, keeping her feet firmly planted on the right spot while she dialed Jan's number.

"How's the cabin?"

She'd missed Jan's throaty voice—she missed hearing any voice. The hours alone in the cabin had been great for her book, but now that Courtney wasn't writing, she missed having company.

"It's remote." Courtney peered out the window next to her, unhinged by the blackness outside. "The cell reception isn't good. if I lose you—"

"And the book?"

Jan's insistence brought a smile to her lips.

"Already working on it. Are you sure about these changes? It seems a bit extreme to me. The story was good before, but what they want—"

Jan's sigh sounded like a siren in Courtney's ears. "Just do the work. Cover everything they want and don't leave anything out. It's a great opportunity for you."

"Is it their book or mine, Jan?"

"It's your book, but they're the ones writing the check for the cover, editing, and all the promo. They get to call the shots."

A twinge of uncertainty erupted in her chest. "Maybe I have better ideas than their editor."

"Girl, please." Jan's obstinance barreled through the speaker. "I know you have better ideas than their editor. A toddler with a crayon could be a better editor than half the people I deal with, but your publisher controls all the strings, and until you get a name, some weight behind that name, and are pulling in six-figures a year, they couldn't care less about your ideas. Just write what they want. We'll fight for your talent and integrity once you hit the bestseller list."

The assertion disheartened Courtney. She believed in Jan, and knew her agent fought for her best interests, she just wished she didn't feel like such a sellout.

"Where are you?" Jan asked.

"Stone Mountain Lodge, outside of Gatlinburg," she told her, keeping the disappointment from her voice. "It was the only cabin I could find."

"I hope you didn't shell out too much. Then again, I might be able to get the publisher to foot part of the bill. Save your receipt."

Courtney's misgivings forgotten, she chuckled. "No, the price was reasonable. Even came fully stocked for the week."

"Wow. Sounds like heaven. When you get back, send me the info. I always keep places like that handy for my writers who need to escape."

"Will do." Courtney fiddled with the deadbolt on the front. "The owner here is great. Peter showed me around and—"

"Peter?" Jan's voice rose. "Is he single?"

"I have no idea." Then Courtney considered how he'd behaved with her, and his invitation to Christmas dinner. "He was a nice guy."

"That doesn't sound good. Stay away from him until you finish this book. I don't need you a mess like with whatshisname. This book requires all your attention, remember that."

There were some things Courtney wished she'd never shared with her agent. The weeks after her ex left, she'd cried to Jan more than once. The tenacious woman had been her lifeline back to the real world. Courtney felt guilty about how she had dominated her time, but as Jan once put it, *"Agents are analysts who get paid by commission."*

"I should let you go." The cold embrace of the cabin surrounded her again. "I'll call with an update soon."

"You do that. And call if you need to talk, too. I'm here for you, Courtney."

Jan hung up and Courtney's loneliness returned. Then her stomach's insistent rumblings drove her to toss the phone onto the sofa and head for the kitchen.

The first place she went was the pantry, wanting to heat up something to chase away the ever-present cold. She rummaged through several cans of soup on the second shelf, disappointed that there was no pea—her favorite. She briefly eyed the boxes of biscuit mix, making a mental note to pull them out in the morning for breakfast.

Her soup selection came down to either the chicken or tomato. Weighing the cans in her hand, she went back and forth until she settled on the tomato.

She searched the counter and then the kitchen drawers for a can opener—nothing. Courtney was about to open one of the overhead kitchen cabinets when a funny sound came from the laundry room.

At first, she brushed the intrusion off as nothing more than the wind picking up. But as time went on, a distinctive grating, almost like claws against wood, grew louder.

Courtney spent years on her family farm and had dozens of encounters with wild animals, but she'd never heard anything like this.

She hunted for a weapon, running through a list of possibilities—raccoon, bobcat, coyote? An uptick in her concern encouraged her to grab the butcher knife from the block on the counter. With the weapon firmly in her grasp, she stood, motionless, straining to make out the uncanny noise.

Scratch. Scratch. Scratch.

It was faint and coming from the back door.

Courtney remained calm, not letting her imagination run wild. The cabin had been off-putting, but what was outside the door came from an animal, and nothing supernatural.

The sound rose again, and she walked into the laundry room. After flipping on the lights, she crept closer to the door, the knife clutched in her hand. The musty smell in the room grew stronger. She wrinkled her nose and then wiped the beads of sweat gathering on her brow.

She stood before the door, checking the security of the deadbolt. Satisfied, she put her ear against the wooden door and waited.

The only thing she could hear was her heart beating in the throat, and then—

Screech.

That was unmistakable. An animal outside, wanting to get in the warm cabin? A branch against the door? Probably. This wasn't human.

Her rational mind told her to walk away and leave whatever was outside alone. Then she heard something that raised a lump in her throat.

"Meow."

No, it couldn't be. Not a cat, out here in this ungodly weather.

"Meow."

The call was stronger and more desperate than before.

Still clutching the knife, Courtney turned the deadbolt. She might not have been an animal person, but she would never leave a helpless creature to die in the cold.

After a firm tug, she cracked the door and peered outside, ready to shut it quickly in case this was something bigger than a cat.

The laundry room light cut into the night and filtered onto the few short steps below the door, but there was nothing there.

Her curiosity waned as the sting of the frigid air cut across her exposed skin. Courtney was about to close the door when a small black nose shoved its way through the crack. Black whiskers followed and then a tall black cat finagled its way in the door.

Her fear melted and pity made her open the door all the way. She knelt. "Well, hello there."

The cat didn't rub against her leg or stop to greet her. The feline bolted inside and hid under her laundry room sink.

Courtney shut the door and set the deadbolt, chiding her silliness. She went to the sink, put the knife aside, and dropped to her knees to get a better view.

Orange eyes, bright and round, stared back at her. This cat was bigger and fluffier than others she'd seen. It had a scruff of dark gray that was rougher than the rest of its smooth black coat. Tall, pointy ears had wisps of gray hair sprouting from the tops like feathers. It had a wide face, a sharp nose, and large paws with thick pads. The feet reminded her of predator cats she'd seen at zoos. It didn't growl or hiss, but calmly stared as if sizing up her intentions.

"I won't hurt you," she said in a hushed voice.

Her words had the effect she'd hoped for. The cat eased out from under the sink, swishing its full tail.

Courtney played with its scruff, marveling at the thick hair. Then she tentatively ran her hand over its back. The silky fur, the immaculate thickness of its coat, and ample plumpness meant the poor creature had not been wild, but probably someone's pet.

"You poor baby. Did you get dumped out here?"

A low, heartbreaking cry, like that of a baby, wiped away all her wariness and she scooped the cat into her arms.

The docile creature purred. Courtney suspected that the cat had known human companionship in the past. Perhaps the lost pet had come to her for help.

She became curious about the sex, especially since the sizable critter was so gentle. Years on her parents' farm had taught her that tomcats were warier of people than queens, but there were always exceptions.

Courtney gently repositioned the calm furball to peek at its rear end.

"You're a girl," she said with a lilt of enthusiasm. "Well, we girls have to stick together."

A fluffy female companion was just the ticket to take away the lingering sense of discomfort the cabin gave her.

She stood, cooing to the giant cat, and carried it to the kitchen.

"We've got to have something here you can eat."

She placed the cat on the counter and opened the fridge. The first thing to catch her eyes was the packets of deli meat.

She checked the contents, and when thick slices of roast beef appeared, she turned to the cat.

"You can eat this. I can't stand roast beef."

She broke the meat up and set the pieces on the counter. But the cat wasn't interested. She didn't even bother to smell the food.

"Wow. You're pretty picky."

Courtney was about to retrieve the milk when the cat jumped from the counter and sauntered over to the Christmas tree, swinging its fluffy black tail.

The animal plopped beneath the tree and stared up at her.

An uneasy flutter erupted in her chest as the animal's orange eyes burned into her. The sensation drifting through her awakened a sense of foreboding. Perhaps taking in the cat hadn't been the best idea.

Courtney shrugged off her concern and returned to her forgotten can of tomato soup. But her appetite had vanished. She brushed a stray lock of hair back into her ponytail while questioning why she felt so ill at ease.

"Enough. It's just a cabin. There's nothing else going on here." She put her hands on her hips and sized up the cat under the tree. "Don't destroy anything. I have horrible memories of barn cats shredding my mother's Christmas ornaments to pieces."

The cat flicked her tail, not appearing the least bit interested in Courtney's house rules.

A fading orange glow from the hearth drew her attention back to the living room. The fire had dwindled. Courtney didn't want to let the flames die. The intermittent crackling and light gave her reassurance. She felt like a child afraid of monsters in the dark, but the thought of losing the firelight left her terror-stricken.

Courtney hurried to set another log atop the fiery red embers.

She was about to return to her laptop when a black shape, dashed outside the living room window.

What the heck was that?

She remained frozen in the living room with her attention focused on the window. There was movement. Something seemed to linger just beyond the porch steps.

This is ridiculous.

Emboldened by a desire to confront her fears, Courtney rushed to the window and put her nose to the glass, squinting into the night.

A tingling careened along her spine, and her heartbeat quickened. Someone waited in the darkness, she was convinced. Courtney shut the window curtains, not wanting to discover if her intuition was right.

"Get a grip. There's nothing out there."

A *thump* from the kitchen startled her. She gasped and pressed her hand to her mouth. Her first thought was that the cat had toppled the Christmas tree.

Courtney ran from the living room, but when she faced the connecting kitchen, she came to a grinding halt.

An older woman in a baggy blue dress opened her kitchen cabinets and appeared to be appraising the contents. A green canvas shopping bag lay on its side atop the counter with green peppers, tomatoes, and a bunch of chives spilling out.

Courtney charged forward. "Who are you? What are you doing in my cabin?"

"Good Lord, dearie." The woman grabbed her chest as she spun around. "You gave me a fright."

Courtney peered through the kitchen to the locked back door in the laundry room. "How did you get in here?"

The round woman tilted her head while giving a cursory inspection of Courtney's figure. The fiery red hair piled atop her head and the pink on her round cheeks glowed in the kitchen light. Her hazel eyes, sprinkled with crow's feet, glinted with hints of amber. Deep creases surrounded her small mouth and lined the creamy skin across her brow.

"Mr. Peter told me you were pretty. I'm glad to see he was right about you."

The knot in her stomach slowly loosened. "You know Peter?"

"I'm Mrs. Finn," she said in a matter-of-fact tone. "I've worked for the Morris family all my life. I'm the cook at the lodge. Mr. Peter asked me to come by and make sure you had a proper dinner."

Courtney inspected her baggy blue dress, noting the modest, full-length sleeves, old-fashioned apron, and high neckline. The black leather shoes peeking out from under her long skirt had pointed toes, laced up the front, and short square heels.

"He sent you out in the freezing cold in that outfit?" She checked the coat rack by the back door. "Where are your snow boots and coat?"

Mrs. Finn chuckled, sounding a little out of breath. "I don't need all that fancy stuff. I'm used to the cold. And you make it sound like Mr. Peter forced me to come here. He did nothing of the kind. I always cook for guests at the lodge, but when he told me about you staying here alone, I came right out to make sure you were all right."

The intact deadbolt on the door puzzled Courtney. "How did you get in? That back door was locked."

"I used my key." Mrs. Finn turned to the fridge. "I have keys to all the cabins."

With the sudden appearance of Mrs. Finn explained, Courtney settled down. She felt guilty about the older woman trekking through the snow to make her dinner but was thankful for the company.

"It was you I saw outside the front window." Courtney suddenly felt foolish for getting so worked up. "I thought ..."

Mrs. Finn turned from the fridge. "Thought what?"

Courtney rested her hip against the kitchen counter. "Never mind. I appreciate you coming all the way from the lodge, but you didn't have—"

Mrs. Finn waved a gnarled hand, silencing her. "I live in a cabin not far from yours, dearie. It's no bother for me to come by. I would rather know you're safe with a warm meal in your belly than worry the night away about you."

Mrs. Finn muttered to herself as she pulled eggs and cheese from the fridge and set them on the counter.

Courtney backed out of the small kitchen, feeling like a bothersome child in the way.

She was grateful, but it had been ages since anyone offered to cook for her. With her days consumed by work and her nights devoted to her writing, she'd been cut off from the world and forgotten how to react to such kindness.

Courtney returned to her laptop on the kitchen table. She sat, and the aroma of the nearby Christmas tree triggered a memory of the cat she'd taken in from the cold.

She glanced under the tree, but the animal was gone. She scoured the dining area and then went to the doorway that led to the living room.

"Mrs. Finn, did you happen to see a cat around here?"

"Oh yes, dearie. The little mouser flew out the door as soon as I came inside."

Courtney went to the breakfast counter, overlooking the dining area. "She got out? She will freeze out there."

Mrs. Finn retrieved a mixing bowl from one of the cabinets below the cooktop. "I wouldn't worry about it. There are lots of cats in these woods. They're Norwegian forest cats. They have more fur than regular house cats and can survive extreme cold. It's said they're favored by the forest spirits. They've been living in these woods as long as anyone can remember."

Courtney didn't buy into the local folklore. "But is the cat tame?"

Mrs. Finn nodded as she cracked an egg. "They're all friendly. They get food from many of the lodgers on the mountain. I even had one as a pet when I was a little girl."

"You grew up here?"

The grind of drawers opening and closing filled the kitchen.

Mrs. Finn retrieved a spoon and looked up at her. "My parents worked for the Morris family, so did my grandparents. My family goes way back in the area."

Her musical way of speaking and her warmth soothed Courtney's misgivings. Comforted by the sounds of the activity in her kitchen, she returned to her computer.

"Mr. Peter told me you're a writer."

Courtney sat behind her laptop, a twinge of curiosity stirring in her. "Peter spoke about me?"

Mrs. Finn offered a beaming smile. Her pointy yellow teeth put Courtney off.

"He said you write books. What kind of books?"

"Romance." Courtney settled back in her chair. "Stories about love and adventure."

"Love?" Mrs. Finn made a face, darkening her bright eyes. "Why would people want to read about that? Romance is silly and always disappoints. People build things up in their heads and wonder why they're heartbroken when everything goes awry. No, good practical stories about people who live interesting lives are what you should be writing. Nothing with all that mushy stuff."

The woman arranged an assortment of vegetables on the chopping block while irritating Courtney with her no-nonsense approach to romance.

"Maybe a lot of people need the escape romance brings," Courtney suggested. "I know my readers want to get away from their lives, not be reminded of them."

Mrs. Finn selected a knife from the block and pointed at her. "You, more than anyone, should know about being led astray by love."

Courtney fidgeted in her chair.

"What makes you say that?" she got out in a tentative voice.

Mrs. Finn cleaved a green pepper in two. "Mr. Peter didn't tell me much, but by the way he spoke, I could guess you're nursing a broken heart." The sizzle of something hitting the hot pan filled the kitchen. "You should learn from that, remember it, and never make the same mistake of trusting a man again. Love leads people astray, and then they can end up in the most terrible places."

Her vehemence turned her voice from uplifting to craggy. The change sent a chill through Courtney.

"What terrible places? Love is uplifting. Love is happiness. Love is—"

"Love is a trap, dearie. The oldest one known to man," Mrs. Finn insisted, her melodic voice returning. "I'm sure your mother would agree with me."

Courtney leveled her focus on her computer, fighting an urge to argue. The cook's strange behavior bothered her, but Mrs. Finn was a trusted employee of the Morris family. No point in getting off on the wrong foot her first night in the cabin.

The blinking of the cursor soon chased away her cantankerous mood. No matter what she felt about Mrs. Finn, Courtney had come to the cabin to write. That was all she had to concern herself with from now on.

Chapter Five

The ham and mushroom risotto whipped up by Mrs. Finn warmed Courtney's insides. No longer uneasy, she set her feet on the coffee table in the living room and admired the dwindling embers in the hearth. A yawn escaped her lips and her eyelids drooped. She folded her arms, longing for a few minutes of sleep before returning to her book.

Mrs. Finn hastily left after cleaning up the kitchen, barely giving Courtney time to thank her for the meal. Courtney thought the Morris family lucky to have such a devoted employee.

Her breathing slowed, and Courtney slipped into a dreamy state. Then the cushion on the sofa next to her dipped.

Courtney bolted upright and gazed around the living room, her heart pounding. Perhaps it was the long day or her fatigue, but she could have sworn someone—or something—had sat next to her.

"Meow."

At her feet, curling its tail around her ankle, the black cat stared up at her with its mysterious eyes.

Her sigh carried around the room as Courtney picked up the cat and held it close.

"How did you get back in here?"

She distinctly remembered locking the back door after Mrs. Finn left. She hadn't seen the cat dart inside.

"You're a sneaky little thing, aren't you?"

The cat purred, and all her questions were quickly forgotten. The reassurance of having another living creature in the cabin mattered more than how the feline had arrived.

Fully awake thanks to the scare, Courtney set the cat down on the sofa and went to add another log to the fire. She had a lot of work to do before heading to bed.

She reached for another log in the copper box next to the hearth only to discover it was the last. Courtney had been dutiful about keeping the fire roaring but hadn't realized she'd gone through that much wood.

She dumped the log on the fire and then pensively eyed the front door. The idea of heading into the night to retrieve more wood didn't sit well with her. Perhaps she could let the fire die. After all, there were plenty of blankets to keep her warm in the cabin.

The cat jumped from the sofa, curled up in front of the fire, and closed its eyes.

The contented creature awakened a pang of guilt. The poor cat had come in from the snow and would appreciate having some warmth. A roaring hearth might also encourage her newfound furry friend to stick around and provide company through the long night.

I guess I'm heading outside.

With a humph, Courtney went to the front door.

On a pine table by the door were three lanterns. Courtney picked up the closest and flipped the *on* switch. The bulb dimly glowed.

She stood before the door, clasping the heavy lantern and finding her courage.

"You're just getting firewood, not fighting off a grizzly."

She wrestled with getting the door open, but after a few quick tugs, the hinges creaked and gave way.

The darkness ate up the light radiating from the house. She put her shoulder into the heavy door, forcing it wider to get the antler chandelier to illuminate the porch. Then the bulbs flickered. Courtney stopped, waiting for the glitch to settle down. When the constant glow from the living room returned to the porch, a frightening apparition appeared before her.

A tall, dark figure approached from the corner of the porch.

A scream climbed the back of her throat. Courtney dashed back inside the cabin and tugged on the door, attempting to keep the unwanted stranger out, but the darned thing wouldn't budge.

The intruder rushed forward, his face and clothes shrouded in black.

She held up the heavy lantern, ready to fling it. "You better think twice about it, buddy."

He came forward, keeping his head down. "Buddy? That's a new one."

The familiar voice created a swell of uncertainty, and she stopped fighting to close the door.

The stranger stepped into the beam coming from inside the door.

His blond hair and the assertive way he carried himself stopped her from throwing the lantern at his head. He carried a bundle of wood and wore a weak smile that lacked the warmth and charm she had seen earlier that day.

"Peter? Is that you?" She lowered the lantern. "What are you doing here?"

He stomped the snow from his boots. "I figured you would be needing firewood about now."

She stared at the wood and then back at his face, aghast. "At this hour?"

He nodded inside the cabin. "Are you going to invite me in or let me freeze?"

She jumped aside, wondering what had possessed him. Maybe he offered the same service to all his lodgers, or did he have another reason for the visit?

He walked into the living room. Courtney got a good look at his clothes as she set the lamp on the table.

"What are you wearing?"

His blue jeans and leather jacket were gone. He had on old-fashioned brown trousers tucked into high-cut black riding boots. His long black woolen coat hung to his calves and appeared as dated and rumpled as his pants and linen shirt.

The cat sprang to life. The hair rose on its back, and then a loud *hiss* drifted through the air.

"What's wrong with you?" she called to the cat.

Courtney watched with dismay as the creature ran from the sofa and into the hallway. When the cat turned toward the bedroom, its back feet skidded on the smooth wood floor, and then it disappeared.

Peter went to the wood box. "You shouldn't let that creature inside. It's vile and probably riddled with disease."

She turned back to him. "She was sweet until you showed up."

He rolled his eyes. "She's only sweet because she wants something from you."

The comment, and the animosity in his voice, set off a flurry of alarm bells in Courtney's head. Perhaps she'd overreacted. She needed to regroup before driving the man away.

She softened her tone and asked, "Why didn't you warn me about the wild cats around here?"

He stacked the logs in the box. "Why would I mention it? You didn't strike me as an animal person."

She ignored the disparaging remark and touched the coarse fabric of his coat. "Are you doing a play or something?"

He stood and wiped his hands. "No. Why do you ask?"

"Those clothes. They look ancient."

He furrowed his brow and then reached for the fireplace poker. "They're warm and a necessity when I have to deliver firewood to young ladies who don't bother to keep an eye on their supply."

The surly tone wasn't like the man she remembered. Perhaps coming out in the cold put him in a bad mood. She regretted being flippant.

"I'm sorry." She folded her hands, attempting to look penitent. "Thank you for bringing the wood. But why are you here? First, you send Mrs. Finn, and now—"

Peter spun around, gripping the poker like a weapon. "She was

62

here?"

"Yeah." Courtney took a wary step back. "She said you sent her to cook dinner for me."

The redness drained from his cheeks. "Ah, yes. I must have forgotten."

He stoked the fire. The *clunk* of the poker jabbing the embers made her uncomfortable. There was something off about him. His affable nature and energy had deteriorated. A scowl replaced the grin she'd found hard to ignore earlier that day.

Peter set another log on top of the flames. She debated what could have brought on such a change.

"Can I offer you a drink? Or there's some of Mrs. Finn's risotto left."

"And how did you get along with the cook?" He peered over his shoulder at her. "Did you like her?"

Courtney moved away from the fireplace, not sure how to phrase her reservations.

"She was very kind to me."

He put the poker back on the brass tool stand. "I hope you didn't say too much to her. She's a notorious gossip."

She folded her arms, giving him an obstinate glare. "That's rich coming from the man who told her I was a writer and came here to recover from a broken heart."

Peter came up to her. "What are you talking about?"

"She could guess by the way you spoke about me that I was nursing a broken heart." Courtney went to the sofa and sat. "Will I be reading about me in the local paper tomorrow, or have you not notified them yet?"

His rigid stance relaxed, and he ran his shaky hand through his hair.

She read frustration in his movements. Part of her was glad to see him ruffled, but another side regretted her candor. The man seemed troubled. A great weight had settled on his shoulders since their first meeting.

"I never said anything to her." His voice softened as he approached her. "She must have heard me speaking to someone else."

The blue wasn't as brilliant in his eyes before. She wasn't sure if it was his boots, or how he hunched his shoulders, but he appeared shorter, too. The lines across his brow and around his mouth were deeper, his jaw wasn't quite as square, and the ruggedness of his features had faded.

"Why are you here, Peter? I could have gotten my own wood."

He went to the opposite side of the sofa, keeping his distance. "You worried me. Coming to this remote cabin the way you did for the holidays … well, it's not something happy people do."

"Happy people?" Her irritation flared. "So you came out here to make sure I didn't kill myself? I guess that could hurt your lodge's reputation."

He sat and let out a long breath. "No, I came because I sensed you needed someone to lean on. It's nothing to be ashamed of. Everyone needs help now and then."

She raised her eyebrows. "I don't. I've overcome a lot of odds to make my way in the world. I'm a successful executive and a burgeoning author, and I've accomplished everything without anyone's help."

Peter tapped the arm of the sofa with a tapered finger, his gaze never wavering. "And that would explain why you're here—alone in an isolated cabin. You refuse to let anyone help you." He stopped tapping and leaned in closer. "It's all right to talk about what's bothering you. Emotions don't make you weak; they make you human."

She was about to argue with him, defend her reclusive lifestyle, and then the fight in her fizzled. He was right—a wound couldn't heal without being tended, and all Courtney had done since getting dumped was ignore her injury. But many people she tried to talk to grew tired of listening.

"No one wants to hear about someone else's problems."

"But I want to hear yours." He sat back, dropping his voice to a gentle murmur. "I want to know what brought you here."

The icy wall that had sprouted around her heart slowly thawed. He might not have been the same kind and considerate man who'd driven her to the cabin, but something was soothing about him. Perhaps the time had come to address the real reason she embraced coming to the cabin.

Her tension retreated as she raised her head to the ceiling, attempting to find the right words.

"When your world falls apart, sometimes all you can register is the destruction and how your feelings gut you. You don't see or hear others when they try to help. It's just noise. But your being here, your kindness, it's made things better. I'm not sure how you did that, but I'm grateful you came out in the cold night to check on me." She wiped her face and stood, uncomfortable with all she'd said. "I'm sure you have other guests to see to."

Peter reclined on the sofa, draping his arm over the back. "What was his name?"

For weeks, she'd refused to say it. Now, she feared speaking his name might give him some power over her.

She sank onto the sofa, twisting her hands.

"Kyle," came out in a long, sad breath.

"And why did you let him break your heart?"

She tossed up her hand. "I caught him with another woman."

"No, that's how your relationship ended." Peter eased closer. "What I want to know is why you let him in? You profess to be strong and not need anyone. What did he have you felt you lacked?"

The question washed over her, creating a funny quiver in her stomach. "I'm not sure how to answer that."

Peter adjusted his coat, getting comfortable. "Try."

She took in his relaxed air, which contradicted his formal attire, and questioned if confiding any more was a wise move. She vacillated between showing him the door and sharing what was on her mind.

"I'm not here to judge, Courtney. Only to listen."

Hearing her name in his smooth, deep voice settled her debate. Perhaps what she needed was an objective opinion.

"When I first met Kyle, he was everything I thought I wanted—intelligent, funny, a man who could make me better." She took a loose lock of her brown hair and twirled it nervously around her finger. "I guess that's what I was looking for—someone who would tell me I was good enough."

He rubbed the golden stubble on his chin. "And did he do

that?"

She let the hair fall from her hand. "I thought he did, but then little things changed my mind. He tore me down most of the time. When we fought, he blamed everything on me. Soon, I became the problem in his life, not the solution. No one was surprised when we ended—not even me."

"Why did you stay with him?"

"Hope, I guess. I didn't want to give up on us."

Peter nodded, and his scowl eased. "Just because he wasn't the right one, doesn't mean you should give up on finding a man who is."

She wasn't sure if it was the roaring fire, the delicious dinner, or his encouragement that sparked her flirty smile.

"What makes you think I've given up?"

He stood and motioned to the door. "I should get back to the main house."

Idiot.

She stumbled to her feet. "Are you sure you will be okay out there?"

"I know this property better than anyone." Peter walked across the living room. "And I'm sure you want to get back to your book."

She stopped halfway to the door. "How did you know I was working on my book?"

"What else would you be doing?"

He opened the door and a biting cold breeze tumbled into the cabin.

"Lock this door after I leave."

Courtney tugged her thick sweater closer. "Why? What could

be out there on such a night?"

He raised the collar of his coat. "You'd be surprised." Peter stepped onto the porch and paused. "Be careful what you say to Mrs. Finn. She can't be trusted with secrets." He pointed at the door.

She tipped her head, keeping her gaze on him as she slowly closed the door. Once she set the deadbolt, Courtney rested her back against the door and sighed.

The furry cat appeared in the hallway, tentatively peering around the living room.

Courtney chuckled. "I came for peace and quiet and ended up getting Grand Central Station."

Chapter Six

*W*arm yellow sunlight filtered through the dining room window and warmed Courtney's back. She stood at the kitchen counter, wrapped in the quilt, and stared at the lifeless coffeemaker. Being denied her freshly brewed cup of morning coffee annoyed the heck out of her.

I'll be sure to mention this in my review.

Courtney's thoughts had never drifted far from her conversation with Peter the night before. She'd replayed portions of it, especially the part where he left abruptly. Did she say or do something wrong? And what was with his strange clothes?

The cat trotted by on its way to the back door. The peculiar feline stopped and looked back at her.

"Do you need to go out?"

She walked across the laundry room, letting the quilt drag on the floor. Courtney had to struggle with the heavy door, but the cat squeezed out before she got it all the way open.

The cat dashed down the steps as the biting cold stinging her face forced her back inside.

Courtney adjusted the quilt around her shoulders and was about to set the deadbolt when the handle rattled. She jumped back, petrified.

The door flew open and banged against the inside wall, sending a shockwave through the laundry room. A burst of wind swept through the door, raising the edges of Courtney's quilt.

Mrs. Finn, wearing another dowdy blue dress and white apron, walked into the cabin as if she owned it. She had no hat or coat, and the only thing she carried was a straw basket covered with a red-checked towel.

Mrs. Finn saw her standing a few feet away and smiled. With a flick of her wrist, the older woman closed the heavy door. The *bang* sent a shudder through Courtney's bones.

How someone Mrs. Finn's age could easily close the same door she'd struggled to open perplexed her.

"Good morning, dearie." Mrs. Finn eyed the quilt. "You're not dressed? It's past ten. You should be up and working on your book."

She warily eyed the older woman. "I won't get anything done without coffee."

Courtney headed back into the kitchen and waved at the idle coffeemaker on the counter. "It's broken."

Mrs. Finn followed her, stomping the snow from her shoes as she went. "Not possible. It's brand new."

Courtney was about to tell her she'd checked the machine twice when Mrs. Finn touched the *on* switch, and the percolator came to life.

A thrill of excitement ran through Courtney when she saw the first drips of coffee filling the pot. "I'm saved."

Mrs. Finn set down the basket. "You shouldn't drink coffee.

It isn't good for you."

"Well, everything is bad for you these days. I might as well enjoy myself before I go."

Mrs. Finn's raspy chuckle floated around the kitchen. The odd sound didn't match the motherly exterior.

"You've got a long time before you have to worry about meeting the dark god."

Her craving for coffee faded. "The dark god?"

Mrs. Finn reached for a coffee mug from the cabinet above the sink. "The dark god is the one who oversees all that is death. He sends his collectors to gather up souls when their time has come to an end."

Courtney pulled her quilt closer. "I've never heard of him."

Mrs. Finn handed her the mug and lifted the coffeepot. "You never want to anger this spirit. Otherwise, he will leave your soul to roam the earth as a ghost."

Courtney snickered while the nutty aroma of the coffee tempted her. "Ghosts don't exist."

Mrs. Finn frowned and put the pot back on the warmer. "They do exist. They are as real as the gods. I know many don't believe in the old ways anymore, but just because you don't believe in something doesn't mean it isn't there." She went to the basket and ripped away the towel, revealing a selection of breakfast muffins. "No, we are never alone on this plane. No matter how much we might like to think we are. Even here, in the dark woods, the spirits are all around us."

"Not something a woman alone in a cabin needs to hear."

Courtney leaned over the basket, inhaling the aroma of the freshly baked muffins. "What gods do you believe in? I mean, other than the dark one."

Mrs. Finn selected a plate from another cabinet. "I'm partial to the goddesses. Strong women who never needed a man to tell them what to do."

Courtney sipped her coffee. "Like the woman carved on the door?"

"Ah, Perchta is very special." Mrs. Finn set the plate next to the basket. "She was said to roam the countryside at midwinter, and to enter homes during the twelve days between Christmas and Epiphany. She would know whether the children had been good and worked hard all year."

"Sounds like Santa Claus."

Mrs. Finn nodded. "In many ways, yes. But Perchta, unlike Santa Claus, has two guises. She would appear as an old crone, haggard and gnarled, to children during the holidays."

Courtney slipped her hands around her mug, engrossed with the tale. "And when she wasn't an old woman?"

"She would appear as a beautiful woman with pale skin and black hair. In that form, she was said to lure men, and a few women, to their death. Then she would trap their souls for all eternity and make them do her bidding."

"She sounds like an imposing witch. Maybe I should search for that book Peter mentioned."

Mrs. Finn's lighthearted chuckle carried around the kitchen. "You don't need the book when you have me. I know all about Perchta."

"Do you know who carved her on that door?" Courtney

lingered over her hot coffee. "Peter said it was the same man who built this cabin."

She plucked a muffin from the basket. "Whoever did it, I'd say they wanted to please Perchta because they chose to show her at her most radiant."

Courtney inspected the fat blueberries atop her muffin. "Isn't that what men do? Put a woman on a pedestal right before they knock it out from under them."

Mrs. Finn brushed a few loose strands of hair from Courtney's face. "The way to protect yourself from falling from that pedestal is to never let a man put you there. No man is worth giving up who you are, who you could be. Sometimes a woman must be alone to realize her greatest potential."

Courtney set her mug down and pinched a blueberry from her muffin. "But even the goddesses end up with someone. No one can be alone forever. Not even the divine."

Mrs. Finn folded her hands. "Perchta never needed a man and neither do you."

Courtney popped the berry into her mouth, still not convinced. "But you're married, right?"

Mrs. Finn went to the freezer. "In my day, women had to marry, but your generation isn't governed by the same norms. You can be anything you want, and what your family desires for you doesn't matter." She opened the door. "I envy you girls today. What I wouldn't give to go back and tell Mr. Finn to pack his bags."

"Doesn't sound like you were very happy." Courtney ripped off a portion from her muffin.

"Happily married is an oxymoron, dearie."

Courtney chuckled, hiding her laughter with her hand. "And where is Mr. Finn?"

Mrs. Finn removed a whole frozen chicken and took it to the sink. "Oh, he died many years ago."

"And do you believe he's roaming the earth as a ghost?"

Mrs. Finn turned to her and winked. "Not if he knows what's good for him."

The succulent aroma of rosemary and roasting chicken drove Courtney to distraction. The lunch Mrs. Finn prepared before she left still had another half an hour in the oven. Courtney had promised not to become distracted by her book and remove the dish promptly when done, but the noises coming from her stomach made work impossible. She moved her laptop from the dining table to the living room, hoping to get away from the mouth-watering smell, but even the smoky essence of the fire in the hearth couldn't mask it.

In the middle of a heated scene, where her heroine accountant first kisses her client, Courtney found herself typing words such as *delicious*, *flavorful*, and *savory*—descriptions better suited to a banquet than a love scene.

She put her laptop aside and decided to open a window, thinking she would rather risk pneumonia than keep writing unusable words.

Before she could open the window, her phone rang.

She went to the sofa and retrieved her phone, before another chorus of the Beyoncé song chimed.

"Hey, checking up on me?"

"That's my job." Jan's acerbic voice filled the living room. "If I send one of my writers to the middle of nowhere, I need to make sure they are still alive and working. I'd feel guilty otherwise."

Courtney snickered, guessing Jan was more worried about the book. "I'm fine. The book is … coming along."

Jan's sigh confirmed Courtney's suspicions. "That's good news because I got a call from the publisher today. They wanted to make sure you were on schedule."

Courtney glimpsed her laptop, a pang of guilt running through her. "I'll be ready."

"I hope you're taking some time for yourself. I don't want to think I'm driving you mad with my crazy deadline."

"I've got people looking out for me here. Peter has someone coming to the cabin and making meals for me—really good ones."

"A cook? Wow." Jan's raucous laughter hurt Courtney's ears. "The guy is trying to impress you."

Courtney stepped toward the kitchen and then stopped. "You're exaggerating. He's being nice."

"Nice is a fruit basket, not a cook."

Courtney was about to argue with her when the lights in the kitchen flickered.

"What's with these lights?"

"What was that?" Jan asked.

A strange whacking sound came from outside her front door.

"Let me call you back." Courtney hung up and hurried to the

front door.

She slid back the deadbolt and cracked the door just as a loud *thwack* cut across the porch. Once on the porch, she stood and listened.

Crack.

The sound came from the side of the house.

Carefully, Courtney descended the porch steps and when her tennis shoes touched the snow, the cold embraced her.

She walked carefully, trying not to slip on the icy patches. Then another *thunk* echoed across the clearing. At a point where the interlocked logs jutted out, she poked her head around the corner.

A man in a long black coat with his back to her held an ax above a stump, ready to bring it down. He swung, and two pieces of cleaved kindling dropped into the snow around the base of the stump.

She inched closer and saw the stacked logs, quartered and ready for the fireplace, against the side of the cabin.

"What are you doing?"

Peter turned to her with the ax gripped in his hand. "You'll need more firewood to get you through until Christmas."

"You came out here to chop wood for me? But yesterday you said I had enough for the coming week."

He dropped the ax and lifted two logs from the ground. "You should go back inside. You're not dressed to be out here."

"And you are?" She gestured to his coat.

He placed the logs on the stack next to the house. "I'm fine."

The breeze picked up and she hugged herself. "Why don't you

come inside?"

He went back and picked up his ax. "I need to finish this."

She waved at the woodpile. "Honestly, Peter, I have enough wood for the apocalypse."

He twirled the ax in one hand, spinning the blade. "A person can never have too much wood in winter."

She could sense his hesitation.

"Mrs. Finn put a rosemary chicken in the oven. You could have lunch with me."

He picked up another log. "I'd rather starve than eat her—" He slammed his lips together and gave her a tentative gaze. "Not hungry."

She cautiously stepped closer, struggling to keep her balance on the slick ice.

Courtney wanted to give the impression that she was a trooper when it came to icy conditions, but before she got within a few feet of him, her right foot went out from under her.

"Whoa!"

She braced for the hard impact, but Peter caught her and pulled her into his arms.

She landed bent over and tipped backward in his arms. They appeared as two dancers caught in a perilous dip.

Her breath rattled around in her chest and heart thundered in her ears. Her almost fall wasn't what made her pulse race.

His face was inches from hers, with a comma of blond hair dipping over his brow. She got a whiff of his musty coat, somewhat disappointed the smell masked his skin. She loved that most about being with a man—their musky, woodsy essence as they pressed against her.

"Are you okay?" His breath was husky and laced with worry.

Keep it together.

"I'm fine."

His powerful arms were nothing like Kyle's. Her ex professed to be an avid kickboxer but always seemed to get out of breath whenever she insisted on taking the stairs. In his arms, she had felt exposed, but with Peter, she felt safe. The way the butterflies in her stomach danced as she gazed into his wintery eyes scared the heck out of her.

Courtney hurried to wiggle her way out of his embrace. She got to her feet, pushing him away.

His face darkened as he took a step backward. "I told you to go back inside. Why don't you ever listen when someone is trying to help you?"

The warmth from her cheeks radiated throughout her body. "You weren't helping me. You were ordering me. There's a difference."

He gave her a half-grin and went back to his ax. "Only to you."

"Maybe if you didn't come across as bossy, I might have listened."

He swung the ax hard, and the blade wedged into the chopping block. "Do you think just because a man suggests that he's being bossy?"

The warmth leftover from his embrace and the fluttering in her belly quickly evaporated.

"Forget it."

She turned back toward the house, wishing she had never set

foot outside. Gingerly, she tested the ice.

Courtney had barely gone two feet when she was suddenly lifted into the air.

She sucked in a loud gasp and came to rest against Peter's chest. He had scooped her into his arms.

She slapped him as she lay cradled against his rock-hard chest. "I can make it back to the porch without you."

"Yes, but by the time you get there, we might freeze to death."

She wanted to call him a bully but didn't. The way he held her, and the peace she felt in his arms, chased away all her reservations.

You're getting enamored. Careful.

Everyone had told her jumping into a relationship soon after the difficult break up could only hurt her more. They were right, she knew that. But what about this man that made her want to throw caution to the wind?

He reached the base of the porch steps and deposited her on the snow-covered ground.

"You should be able to handle the rest."

His curt tone rattled her. Shades of the cheery man she'd met after arriving at the lodge contrasted sharply with the dour, grumpy person in front of her. Even his eyes had lost their sparkle. They felt as cold as the wind whipping around them.

"You didn't need to do that."

"I know, but I did anyway." He motioned up the steps. "I'll bring some more wood inside for you."

"Why are you different?" She tipped her head, taking in the set of his mouth. "Yesterday you were nice and now you're …" She motioned at his clothes.

"Do you prefer me that way?"

The fight in her retreated, and her body sagged. "It's not a question of liking you one way or the other. I want to know why you feel … angry all the time."

His shoulders lost their stiffness, his face relaxed, and a wisp of a grin teetered across his taut mouth.

"I'm sorry if you think I'm angry at you. I'm not. I want to protect you from things—" His grin disappeared. "Things that can hurt you."

"I'm a lot tougher than I look."

He nodded. "Everyone usually is."

She shook her head and headed up the steps. She stomped across the porch boards, frustrated.

Courtney put her hand on the doorknob, taking in the beautiful woman's face captured in the wood.

"What things?" She glanced back at him. "What things can hurt me?"

He blew out a loud breath and slowly climbed the steps. "That might be hard to explain."

She opened the door. "Then you'd better come inside and try."

Chapter Seven

The cold seeped through her sweater, and she couldn't feel her toes. Courtney stood on the porch and glared back at Peter, unsure about what infuriated her more—his constant broodiness, or his overprotective streak. Either way, the man had wormed his way under her skin, and she didn't like it.

She took a step inside the cabin. A *whoosh* of black dashed past her legs. She stopped and tracked the movement of the furry cat.

The creature jumped on the sofa and circled. When Courtney stepped over the threshold, the beast stared at her with its creepy eyes.

Peter came up behind her. "I told you to not let that cat inside."

Courtney kicked off her wet shoes. "It's just a cat. Or is she one of those things that can hurt me?"

Peter raised his head, sniffing. "Is something burning?"

Icy dread rolled through her. She raced from the door and headed to the kitchen.

Smoke broached the divide between the rooms.

"I forgot about Mrs. Finn's chicken!"

Courtney dashed toward the oven. When she flung the door

open, a thick, black cloud billowed out.

She waited for the piercing scream of a fire alarm as she searched the counter for a towel to grab the casserole dish.

Peter was at her side, pushing her out of the way. "Good thing I carried you back to the cabin, otherwise the whole place could have gone up."

She found a towel, but he'd already lifted the chicken out of the oven with his bare hands.

"What are you doing?"

He dumped the dish with the chicken into the sink.

She took his hands, examining his palms. "That was a stupid thing to—"

There wasn't a burn or red mark on him. Already on edge from Mrs. Finn's peculiar conversation earlier, Courtney spiraled into a rabbit hole of unnatural causes for Peter's escaping injury.

"How did you do that?"

He yanked his hands away. "No harm done."

A cold swath cut through her as she stood by the sink, questioning what she'd seen. "You should be burned."

He held up his hands and then used his fingers to lift the sleeves of his coat to cover his palms.

"Aren't you glad I wore my old black coat."

The silly grin on his face filled her with a mixture of relief and amusement. She laughed and leaned against the sink.

Peter narrowed his gaze. "What's so funny?"

She waved her hand, reining in her giggles. "For a split second, I thought you weren't human or something. Blame Mrs. Finn and her ghost stories."

"What did she say?"

Courtney inspected the chicken, hoping some portion remained salvageable. "Some crazy story about a dark spirit collecting the souls of the dead. How spirits are everywhere, even in these woods. You should hire her to tell ghost stories to your guests."

He chuckled, filling the kitchen with a cool, gravelly sound.

Even his laugh is different than before.

"If Mrs. Finn spoke to the guests, there would be no more business." He poked at a charred chicken leg. "She even scares me most of the time."

A blur of black shot down the hallway. The frights of the day must have taken their toll because Courtney didn't jump or scream. She simply eased away from the sink and followed the suspicious sight to the dining area.

Under the Christmas tree, the cat, its head hidden in a few of the green branches, set its unsettling eyes on her.

She knelt to get a better look. "You're a funny little girl, aren't you, sweetie?"

"You should toss that beast outside."

She stood and faced Peter, scowling. "It's just a helpless animal. How can you be so cruel?"

A hiss rose from the base of the tree.

"See?" She waved to the cat. "You've upset her."

Peter came around the kitchen counter, no longer appearing concerned about the cat, but frowning at the small fir tree.

"Why haven't you decorated your Christmas tree?"

Courtney went back to the kitchen counter, bewildered by the agitation she detected in his voice. "I doubt I'll get around to decorating it."

He went to the yellow boxes filled with decorations on a corner of the dining table. "You have to do something. It's bad luck to leave a tree undecorated."

She pushed away from the counter, smirking. "Bad luck? Since when?"

The cat dashed out from under the tree and took off down the hallway, heading toward the bedroom.

Peter stepped closer to the tree. "Growing up, my family was always adamant about decorating the tree as soon as we got it inside. My mother told me stories about the Yule tree and how it was brought inside to provide a warm and festive place for the spirits who inhabited the woods. To not decorate the tree and welcome the spirits to the celebration would incur their wrath. They would send the Yule Cat to seek vengeance."

"Yule Cat?" Courtney let slip a snicker and then covered her mouth.

"The Yule Cat is a huge and vicious creature who lurks about the snowy countryside during Yuletide and eats people who do not share in the festivity of the season." Peter stood next to the tree, rubbing the end of one of its branches between his thumb and forefinger. "Many cultures across Europe have similar variations of the Yule Cat, and all are based on the same principle—misfortune befalls those who refuse to carry the joy of the season in their hearts."

She attempted to put on a serious face before she said, "You sound as bad as Mrs. Finn and her crazy story about that witch."

He turned to her, wearing a deep scowl. "You shouldn't laugh. For many, Perchta isn't a story, but someone to fear."

"Aw, come on. Yule Cats, witches—these are fairy tales made to scare children."

The left side of his mouth curled upward in a half-grin. "I'm curious. What did she tell you about Perchta?"

She walked up to him. "How she had two forms—one that terrorized children, and another that bewitched men."

"She lured men to their death," he corrected as his hint of a smile vanished. "And after, the victim's soul would be held hostage in a dark forest. A sinister place where she could torture them with the hope of release and taunt them with her cruelty." He glanced at the dining area. "You should learn more about her. One should always be prepared to confront the unexpected."

"The unexpected?" This time she didn't hold back her chuckle. "Are you suggesting the witch carved into my front door will come to life?"

He inched closer to her. "No, but Perchta represents the dark forces that can suddenly overtake a person, obliterating the good they once believed in."

She wasn't sure if it was the way he told his tale, in a voice that oozed foreboding, or the sunlight from the window catching in his dusky blue eyes, but there was something about him that fascinated her.

The sorrow, which he carried like a heavy mantle, felt more poignant than ever. He seemed carefree and filled with life when they'd first met.

"What happened to you? What makes you go from being such

a happy guy to the purveyor of gloom?"

His eyebrows went up. "Purveyor of gloom?"

She lifted the lapel of his coat with her forefinger as if inspecting the fabric. "Well, you're not exactly overflowing with Christmas cheer, are you? Even your puritanical clothes give off a real downer vibe. Do you ever lighten up and become that guy I met at the lodge? Or is that all for show?"

His back stiffened. "Do you prefer that man to me?"

She tossed her head, flipping her loose ponytail around her shoulder. "Well, he sure would be more fun at a Christmas party than you."

The smidgen of light in his face died, turning his features into a glum mask. "If that's how you feel, I won't come here anymore."

He was about to move past her when she grabbed the sleeve of his coat. "I'm not saying this to drive you away. I'm trying to get you to enjoy yourself a little more. You're always so serious." She let go of his coat. "What do you do for fun?"

He glowered at her. "Fun isn't on the agenda."

"Well, what about Christmas? What do you do at the holidays to bring that 'joy of the season' into your heart? Since you seem to think I'm lacking holiday spirit, what would you suggest I do to find it?"

He took a step back, sizing her up with his gaze. "First, I'd put something on your tree. Anything. And if you don't like the decorations sent to you, then make your own. You could put something on paper. In old times, children would draw pictures of their hopes for the coming year and place them on their tree. Perhaps a piece of fruit, which symbolizes a successful harvest. Or

86

you could add coins, which represent wealth."

She rolled her eyes. "Decorate the tree or else end up cat food. Yeah, I got that."

His brows came together. "How's your singing voice?"

"Worse than my holiday spirit." She held up her palm and flexed her fingers, encouraging him to keep going. "What else?"

"What about a sleigh ride?"

She shook her head. "I'm an indoor girl."

"Baking Christmas cookies?"

She pointed to the sink. "After what I did to Mrs. Finn's chicken? Are you crazy?"

The grim line returned to his lips. "What did you do when you were a child to celebrate?"

A vise of cold, more daunting than the weather, cinched her chest, nearly sucking the air from her lungs.

She took a few steps backward, no longer interested in their game. "I need to get back to my book."

He stuck close to her, not allowing her to get away. "Courtney, please. Stop asking me to reveal everything about my life when you're not going to share yours with me. You can't help me unless you let me help you."

A wave of molten anger bubbled through her, chasing away the cold. "Who says I need help?"

He ran his finger under her chin, raising her eyes to his. "You're here alone at Christmas, you won't decorate your tree, and you're very suspicious of those who try to help you. That's enough to choke a Yule Cat."

She could not help but smile.

He removed his finger. "Talk to me and let's see if we can find a way to make things better for both of us."

Her anger retreated, leaving behind a swell of regret. There were many things she'd denied herself in the past, including happiness. Perhaps Peter had the right idea—talking through all the self-recrimination might lift the weight on her heart.

Her fingers twisted as she summoned her courage to relive the past.

"Christmas was always a big deal with my family. My mother goes all out every holiday. She loves to embarrass me every year with ugly sweaters." She sucked in a deep breath, fighting a flood of homesickness. "But this year, I couldn't take being around my family and pretending to be happy."

He folded his arms. "Do you have any siblings?"

She went to the counter and leaned against it. "A brother, Matt. He's younger than me and a great guy. You can't help but like him. He has all my mother's optimism."

"What about your father?"

Courtney paused. "My real dad left when I was five. The last Christmas we shared we decorated the tree together. I can still hear the way he laughed as Matt tried to hang an ornament when he could barely stand—he was two at the time. What is still vivid in my memory is the moment he lifted me up to put the star on top of the tree, I ..." She hugged herself. "Well, I've never felt as special with anyone again. Not long after the divorce, my mother remarried my stepfather, Gerald Winston. He's very kind, a lot like my mother, and loves me and my brother. He even adopted us."

"What did your father say about that?"

"Don't know." She sniffled as a lump formed in her throat. "No one heard from him after he left. I think my mother knows where he went, but she's never said a word."

Peter inched closer, dipping his head. "And what about Christmas with your stepfather? Did he like to celebrate the season?"

"Gerald loves Christmas almost as much as my mother. My mother plans lots of parties, hot chocolate drinking contests, has tons of presents under the tree, and dinner consists of more food than we can eat. Sometimes I think she tries so hard to make up for not having my dad around. Even when there wasn't a lot of money, she always made Christmas a big deal."

Peter sighed and placed his hands on his hips. "You could be with your family now, celebrating and drinking hot chocolate."

"Oh, no! I'm not going near my family. Matt just married the perfect girl according to my mother and the last thing I need is to listen to how successful my brother was in finding a wife and when am I going to find a husband. Staying here is easier on my nerves."

"But it's not making you happy. You could tell them how you feel, and that you will find a man when you're ready. Get the hard stuff over with and then you can enjoy those traditions you share. They may not like what they hear from you, but they're your family—they will understand."

She arched an eyebrow. "What about your family? I noticed you haven't mentioned them."

He went around her to the kitchen. "They left me behind long ago."

She tensed, curling her hands. "But you said they were coming to the lodge for Christmas dinner. You even invited me to meet them."

He stopped at the sink but didn't look at her.

"I meant, they have long moved away and left me to run this place alone. I never see much of them anymore."

She walked up to him, studying his rigid posture. "You don't sound any different from me. We've both left our families and find them awkward to return to. At least you have Mrs. Finn to care for you."

He faced her, his scowl deepening. "I prefer to keep my distance from her."

She leaned back against the counter, weighing the simmering contempt she heard in his dark voice.

"What makes you say that? She's been with your family for years. She's so devoted. I thought you sent her to me because you trusted her."

"She's a difficult woman and has a foul temper, which creates a lot of tension between us, but she is a good cook." He rubbed his hands together, the animosity in his voice fading. "And it's not devotion that keeps her tied to this place. She has other motivations."

"Like what?"

He put his hands to his sides and straightened his shoulders. "I suggest you ask her that question. We aren't speaking to each other at the moment."

Courtney spent years growing accustomed to the highs and lows endured by employers and employees. Volatility was the norm in most business relationships and considering Mrs. Finn's twisted views, she was sure Peter's annoyance was probably well-founded.

"Well, if Mrs. Finn had her way, she would want me to remain single all my life. Which is sounding better the older I get. Imagine the money I can save on dating apps."

"She isn't an authority on love," he returned in a scornful tone. "Far from it. Find someone to hold on to and ignore Mrs. Finn's advice. You deserve to be happy."

"Me? I sometimes think that fairy tale passed me by ages ago."

He grabbed her shoulders, almost shaking her. "Listen to me. You're a beautiful woman and will make a man very happy someday. Don't let your past eat at you, or you will end up no better than Mrs. Finn or me."

An uncomfortable silence lingered in the air.

Courtney wasn't sure how to interpret his unwavering belief. A testament to his feelings for her, or was this some friendly advice? *This is why I can't find anyone. I'm terrible at reading signals.*

He let her go. "I should get back to work."

"But what about our lunch?" She glimpsed the chicken and grimaced. "I can make something else. I'm a whiz with club sandwiches."

He waved off her offer. "I have things to attend to. Some other time."

Peter headed to the laundry room, appearing eager to make his escape. She rested her shoulder against the entrance to the room and waited as he unlocked the deadbolt and easily pulled the heavy door open.

"Thank you for listening to me," she said as the frigid air entered the room. "And I don't prefer the Peter you were when we first met. I like you the way you are, funny clothes and all."

The harsh line on his lips lifted and a small smile deepened the sharp curve of his sleek cheekbones. The effect gave his face some much-needed warmth. Then the hollowness that haunted his features returned, and the coldness rose in his eyes.

"Thank you, Courtney. I promise to be merrier the next time I come to visit."

Before she could reply, he slipped through the door and pulled it closed.

The emptiness of his absence added to the chill that constantly hounded her. Courtney fantasized about getting closer to Peter, but the outside world would demand her return. She would have no choice but to leave him behind and get back to her job, her agent, and the broken pieces of her life.

Chapter Eight

The warm glow from the fire bounced off the log cabin walls as Courtney sat curled on the sofa beneath her quilt, the black cat asleep next to her. Her eyes glazed over. She blinked at her computer screen, overcome with fatigue. The words she'd written made no sense, and her frustration with her floundering story made her want to hurl the laptop into the hearth.

She slapped the computer lid closed, fearing she would have to delete the entire story. The modern-day tale of a woman fighting to keep her career and love life alive sounded stale and flat the more she reread it. What had the publisher liked about it?

They didn't like it. That's why you're rewriting it.

The thump of the cat's tail roused her from her worries. The animal's wary eyes peered around the cabin. After stretching out its front paws, the furry feline leaped to the floor.

It trotted toward the kitchen, appearing to not have a single care, and disappeared behind the counter.

She admired its calm demeanor and wished she could be as impervious to stress.

"Yeah, well, that cat knows nothing of deadlines."

The thump of the back door made Courtney grab at her chest.

She put her computer aside and considered the fireplace poker.

"Hello, dearie," came from the kitchen.

Courtney slumped and after shaking her head, wiggled out from under her quilt.

When she arrived in the kitchen, Mrs. Finn greeted her with a frown and a gnarled finger pointing at the disaster waiting in the sink.

"What did you do to my chicken?"

Guilt engulfed Courtney. She silently berated herself for not tossing the offensive fowl into the forest for the animals to feast on.

"I'm sorry." She wrung her hands. "I forgot. By the time I got to it, the chicken was burnt to a crisp."

"Child, that's not burnt, it's cremated." Mrs. Finn set her green canvas bag by the sink. "Might as well chuck it outside for the animals."

"I was going to do that, but then I got caught up in my book."

Mrs. Finn grinned at her, showing off her discolored teeth. "Sounds like things are progressing nicely with your novel. Glad to hear you are getting some work done."

Courtney went to the counter and slumped against it. "Not really. I can't seem to make it come together. The more I read it, the more I realize the story isn't there."

Mrs. Finn dug a few potatoes from her bag. "Perhaps you're trying too hard. Isn't a story supposed to flow out of you?"

Courtney sighed. "Yeah, but this one isn't. I think I'm stuck."

Mrs. Finn put her hands on her hips and stared at the chicken. "Well, if your book wasn't responsible for burning my chicken, what was?"

Courtney went around the counter and peered down at the blackened bird. "I was outside talking to Peter."

"Must have been some conversation." Mrs. Finn lifted the pan from the sink. "What were you two talking about?"

"Christmas mostly." Courtney crossed her arms, wishing she still had her blanket around her. "We spoke about what we used to do with our families at Christmas."

"I'm surprised he mentioned his family. It's a bit of a sore spot with him."

The information raised a tingle of concern in Courtney. "How so?"

"It's not like me to spread gossip." She reached for a towel and wiped her hands. "But Peter and his brother had a falling out over a girl. She belonged to his brother, Lawrence, the eldest who inherited the family fortune, but Peter fell in love with her. Almost tore the brothers apart."

Courtney's ears perked up. Any insight into Peter's demeanor, no matter the source, was welcomed.

"What happened?"

Mrs. Finn adjusted her apron. "She married Lawrence. He got all the Morris money and Peter was given this lodge to run. Poor boy was heartbroken."

Guilt squeezed her insides. The whole time she'd been lamenting her heartbreak but had never considered Peter's.

"I never let go of any woman. They let go of me."

"He mentioned something when we first met, but I never realized how devastated he might have been. He seemed upbeat at the time. But lately, Peter has been down. He's a tough guy to pin

95

down."

"He was always such a moody child, especially around the holidays. He would change his mind frequently about what he wanted and then be crestfallen when he didn't get it." Mrs. Finn took the potatoes to the sink. "I'm not surprised that he didn't fight for the woman he loved."

The comment took Courtney off guard. "What do you mean fight for her?"

She flipped on the tap and put the potatoes under the running water. "Her name was Evelyn. She was the daughter of a friend of the Morris family. Pretty, sweet girl, and just as in love with Peter as he was with her. She didn't want to cause a falling out, so she married Lawrence." Mrs. Finn reached over to a drawer and retrieved a potato peeler. "But if Peter would have stood up to his family, told everyone how he felt about her, Evelyn might be his wife now and not Lawrence's."

A sick, burning rose in the back of her throat. "But why didn't he? To think that he loved her, and she him, is horrible. Imagine how happy they would have been together. That seems so tragic."

Mrs. Finn attacked one potato with the peeler, letting the skin tumble into the sink. "Perhaps it's for the best. The feud could have torn the family apart. Such turmoil isn't in anyone's interest."

Mrs. Finn's cool appraisal sickened Courtney. To cheer against love wasn't in her being. It was one of the quirks of writing romance—love always had to win in the end.

She stared at her computer on the sofa in the next room, a

plan percolating.

"I wonder what would have happened if they ended up together?"

"There would have been turmoil in the family for sure. No, Evelyn made the right decision." Mrs. Finn turned off the water. "She's happy with Lawrence."

Courtney eyed the older woman, amazed by her pessimism. "I can't believe that. I won't believe that. Love should never be wasted like that. Maybe I can find a way to give them their happy ending."

The creases on Mrs. Finn's brow deepened. "What on earth are you talking about, dearie?"

"Just thinking like a writer, Mrs. Finn."

Courtney walked out of the kitchen and was about to pass the Christmas tree when she remembered Peter's warning. The bare limbs nagged at her. Perhaps she should do something. The last thing she needed was the anger of some crazy woodland creatures or a disappointed Peter getting in the way of her work.

I should appease everyone, just in case.

"Do you have an apple or a piece of fruit in your grocery bag?"

Mrs. Finn frowned. "No, why? Did you want fruit?"

Courtney motioned to the tree, warming to the idea of decorating it. "Peter told me this tale about angering the fairies or nymphs or whatever there are in the forests by leaving my tree undecorated. He mentioned something about a tradition where you put fruit or coins on the branches. Thought I'd give it a try."

Mrs. Finn let out a harsh cackle that grated against Courtney's skin. That the sweet, older woman could make such a hideous noise unnerved her.

"That boy was always the imaginative one. Lawrence was the thinker, but Peter was the dreamer. I'm surprised he didn't become a writer like you."

A nugget of doubt took hold of Courtney. "He said the tale came from Europe."

Mrs. Finn took her potatoes from the sink to the chopping board. "There's no such thing. The only fairy creatures I know living in a tree work for the Keebler Company. Probably where he got the idea from."

"But you believe in ghosts and spirits in the woods? How is that any different than what Peter shared with me?"

"Because ghosts are real. People have been seeing spirits for centuries. In modern times, we have video capturing their essence." Mrs. Finn sliced into one of the potatoes. "As far as I know, no one has captured a fairy on film."

"And what about the Yule Cat?" Courtney's support for Peter floundered. "He said it devours those who don't have the Christmas spirit."

Mrs. Finn nodded at the back door. "What nonsense. Perhaps he got the idea from your furry friend who dashed out the door when I came in?" Her snicker rolled around the kitchen. "Maybe you should have him help you with your book."

Courtney left Mrs. Finn in the kitchen and headed to the living room, eager to get down a few notes on her new story idea.

The woman's troubling negativity began to chafe against the romance writer inside her. If most of the world believed as Mrs. Finn, then her business wouldn't be as big as it was. She couldn't understand where the older woman's bleak attitude came from, but Courtney was thankful that not all of her negativity had rubbed off on Peter. There was still hope in his heart, she could feel it, and now that she knew the cause of his sadness, she would try to raise his dismal spirits.

Chapter Nine

$\mathcal{A}$ thick sheet of ice covered the bedroom window, persuading Courtney to stay beneath her warm covers until spring. Then the memory of the new story she outlined had her itching to return to her computer. She remained in bed, staring at the wooden beams in the ceiling and plotting out the first few scenes of her new book. A mild snoring interrupted her thoughts. She turned to see the black cat curled into a ball by her feet, appearing as content as she felt under her pile of blankets.

The animal had stuck close to her since coming inside when Courtney checked the lock on the back door before bed. The fluffy furball stayed with her as she wrote and slept, taking away her unease about the cabin and lessened her loneliness.

Maybe Mrs. Finn is right. I need a cat, not a man in my bed.

But the cook's unflappable distaste for love still did not sit well with Courtney. She had met a few naysayers in her time, but none harbored the animosity of Mrs. Finn. The woman's toxic attitude made her wonder what happened to turn the woman off love.

Courtney was about to shove her blankets aside and brave the cold in her bedroom when she spied something on the bedside table. A sketch of a beautiful woman with flowing hair graced the cover of a book. She didn't remember placing the hardback there before she went to sleep.

She picked up the tome, and a sense of recognition flooded her. The portrait was the same as the woman carved into the front door—Perchta.

"The Witch of Winter," she murmured while reading the title.

Curious, she turned on the lamp next to her and slipped through a few pages until something made her stop.

"To some, she is 'Berchta' and in Russia 'Baboushka.' The Italians call her 'La Befana,' but to everyone, she is a master of witchcraft. Unlike most witches of legend, Perchta has many guises and is most popularly known as a crone who taunts ungrateful children at Christmas. But her lesser-known likeness is of the younger beautiful woman. This is Perchta at her most evil."

Courtney licked her lips, captivated by the story, but also unsure about continuing. The last thing she needed was to fuel her fear.

She debated putting the book aside, but her curiosity won out. When she turned the page, she discovered another interesting passage.

"Perchta lives in forests, surrounded by animals, and often transforms into a large black cat. Men are her favorite victims, although there have been reports of women coming under her powers. She preys on the brokenhearted, encouraging them into dangerous circumstances that invariably end their lives. Once dead, she holds these souls captive, keeping them trapped in a perpetual state of misery. To free themselves from her grip, a soul must make a great sacrifice. One that is fraught with danger and the possibility of eternal damnation."

The bedside lamp flickered, and the cat jumped to attention. The fur on its back, and the black ruff around its neck, stood on end.

Courtney flinched and slammed the book closed. "What is it?"

The cat leaped from the bed, making the mattress shake.

"Hey." Courtney tossed the book aside and climbed from the bed.

The cold cabin air tickled her bare skin. She reached for her robe, desperate to get warm.

The cat scurried from the room and headed down the hall.

"Where are you going?"

She followed the cat, a nervous stitch in her belly, while she fumbled with getting her arms through the sleeves of her robe.

She reached the kitchen and listened again.

The cat ran to the living room.

Courtney followed, scrambling to keep up, her heart beating frantically as she peered out the closest window. Frost covered the glass, making it impossible to look outside.

The cat jumped, batting at the doorknob. The feline appeared larger stretched out against the dark wood. Courtney had never felt intimidated by its size, but as the stories of the Norwegian cats haunting the forests, and Peter's scary tale of the Yule Cat floated through her head, her edginess got the better of her.

She reached for the door and quickly drew back the deadbolt. "Okay, I'll let you out."

The cat swiped at her hand, seeming desperate to get outside.

Courtney tugged hard at the door. She strained, putting all her weight into it. The cat shot out as soon as it could squeeze through and ran across the porch.

"What are you doing?"

Peter's face popped in the narrow opening, scaring her to death.

She jumped back. "You frightened me."

He grinned through the crack in the door. "Why? Who else would come out here on a freezing morning to check on you?"

She was about to explain how the book on Perchta spooked her, but Courtney didn't want to come across as anything less than plucky and independent.

"I wasn't expecting anyone. That's all."

"Your door is stuck with ice. Stand back while I free the bottom up."

She pulled the lapel of her robe closer to her chest and made sure the belt was cinched tight, then she fretted about how horrid she must look after a long night of writing.

A *thud* shook the living room. She stepped back, searching the room for a mirror—any reflective surface would do. Then she caught a brief snippet of her reflection in the brass fireplace tools.

Good enough.

She went to the hearth right as another loud bang rang out.

"Almost there," Peter called.

Courtney gripped the fireplace shovel, amazed by the shine on it. She checked her reflection in the brass blade.

Oh, for the love of God.

The right side of her head had what looked like a bird's nest in it. The way her long hair bunched and stood to the side elicited a groan. She quickly ran her hand through her hair, attempting to smooth the jumble.

A booming *crack* reverberated throughout the cabin, sending a chill down her spine.

"There," Peter cried out with more than an inkling of pride. "Got it."

She heard the thud of the front door closing and shoved the shovel behind her as she spun around to greet him.

He thumped the snow from his boots as he observed her, leaving chunks of mush melting on her floor.

"What are you doing?"

The pensive line on his brow and the way he glared at her made her want to sink into a hole in the floor and never come out.

"Nothing," she said, slipping the shovel behind her.

He came up to her. "What are you hiding?"

With his bounding stride, he was quickly on her and wrestling to retrieve the shovel from behind her back.

She dipped and swayed to keep the shovel out of his hands. "Peter, it's nothing."

His arms were too long for her. After he snatched the shovel away, he lifted it in the air.

"Why do you have this? Were you going to hit me with it?"

"No!" She kept her face hidden and she snatched the shovel back. "I was cleaning the hearth." She set the shovel back with the other fireplace tools.

Peter touched her shoulder, encouraging her to look at him. "Why aren't you telling me the truth?"

She sighed, letting her shoulder droop. There was no way she could hide her morning uglies.

She raised her head, letting him get the full treatment.

"If you must know, I was trying to fix my hair." She patted her unruly mane of hair. "You just showed up and never gave me the chance to brush my hair or"—she put her hand over her mouth—"brush my teeth."

He scratched his head, his lips twisted into a grin. "There's nothing wrong with your hair." He leaned in closer. "Or your breath."

She took a step backward. "Why don't I believe you?"

He chuckled at her stony gaze. "Get dressed while I make us some coffee. You'll need to bundle up for where we're going."

She arched an eyebrow. "And where is that?"

He grinned at her, looking nothing like the pensive man she had come to know.

"We're going to have some fun."

Chapter Ten

$\mathcal{I}$ ce crystals, hanging from tree limbs, caught in the sunlight as Courtney walked the short path. The snow crunched below her boots as the brisk air stung her exposed skin, but the clear blue skies bewitched her. Trees, their limbs heavy with snow and ice, appeared like old women, bent over and pained with their burdens. Cardinals, bluebirds, and yellow finches, their brightly colored feathers standing out against the snow, serenaded her with happy songs as she passed beneath their branches.

A red fox darted out from behind some rocks, his fuzzy red tail and black feet enchanting Courtney. Above, a red hawk searched for its next meal. And squirrels, their bushy gray tails flicking, dashed up and down tree trunks as she passed.

"Which way are we heading?" she asked. "I'm getting turned around."

Peter pointed his right hand at the sun. "It's still morning. The sun is in the east." He pointed his other hand in the opposite direction. "And that is west. So, the way I'm facing is south. Head south anywhere on this land and you will either run into a road or the lodge."

She peered into the forest ahead. "But we're heading north."

He started back down the path. "North takes you deeper into the property."

She followed him, gazing at the sky. "It's beautiful. I don't think I've ever seen the sky so blue."

"You miss such things in the city. The sky, the animals, the snow on the trees and ground."

"When the snow is this heavy, the plows get to it before anyone else. Most mornings there's only slush on my street, nothing like this."

Peter strolled beside her with his coat collar pulled up around his neck. "How long have you lived in Nashville?"

"Since my mother moved us there to marry Gerald. I'm from Memphis originally."

Peter knocked an icicle from a branch next to him. "I've never been there."

"Where did you grow up?"

"Knoxville. My family had a sawmill on the Tennessee River but got out of the business and started buying up land. They have real estate holdings all over the state, but they gave me this property in the hopes of attracting vacationers from the bigger cities wanting to get away."

"Like me."

He nodded. "When I took over, I worked hard to get this retreat organized." He glanced at a passing cardinal. "There was a lot to do. Looking back, everything seemed so challenging."

She shoved her hands behind her back, itching to ask about Evelyn. "Why aren't you overseeing the real estate they own? Why send you here?"

The change in his mood felt like a dark cloud descending. She chastised her selfish curiosity.

"I don't want to pry," she quickly added. "But you seem like a smart and capable man."

He stopped walking and kicked at a snowdrift. "My parents didn't think I was smart and capable. Also, I wasn't the oldest." He sighed and his lips turned downward. "My older brother, Lawrence, got to run the family investments. We had a falling out and when the time came, I chose to come here. I didn't want to be around him or his new wife."

She eased under his lowered head. "Why not?"

"I did something foolish. I fell in love with my brother's fiancée—Evelyn."

Courtney felt terrible for coaxing the information out of him, but also relieved. If he could share his past with her, then, perhaps, he trusted her.

"And is she the reason you live out here alone?"

He started down the path again. "I'm not alone. I have the staff, and the guests who stay at the lodge."

"And Mrs. Finn," she added.

He tossed back his head and groaned. "Don't remind me."

His reaction baffled her. "What is the deal with you two?"

Peter kept walking, forcing her to keep up with his long stride. "I don't like busybodies." His flat tone shocked her. "She causes trouble most of the time."

"But she is a great cook," Courtney said, coming to her defense.

He gave her a funny side-glance that put her teeth on edge.

The mixture of animosity and resentment she saw in his gaze told her to not push.

"People are never as they appear."

The comment confused her. Did he mean Mrs. Finn or her? Courtney wasn't sure. She decided to change the topic of the conversation, hoping to lighten the mood.

The path narrowed and dipped downward. She had to watch her step on the slick ground. The base of the trees around them became clogged with brush, obliterating her views of the forest. The blue in the sky disappeared behind a canopy of interlaced branches topped with snow. The songs of the birds, the whisper of the wind, and the life around them vanished.

A trickle of apprehension tightened her gut. "Where are you taking me?"

She hesitated when a large branch dipped before her, almost blocking the way.

Peter lifted the branch, beckoning for her to continue.

"Someplace magical. You'll see."

The growing darkness in the tunnel concerned her. She was not one to suffer from claustrophobia, but if the end didn't appear soon, Courtney feared she might insist they return to the cabin.

But then a twinkle of light, like the sun reflecting on ice, danced up ahead. The way the glimmer bobbed and weaved hypnotized, encouraging her forward.

The trees around them lifted, and the tunnel widened, allowing the sun to peek through. The heavy brush receded, and Courtney sighed with relief when she could see across the forest once again.

The path took a steep turn downward. She reached for a tree to keep from slipping on the muddy slush.

"Here." Peter took her hand, helping her along.

They came to a low-hanging branch, heavy with snow, and Peter brushed it aside, allowing them to pass.

When she stepped behind the branch, Courtney sucked in an astonished gasp.

The path ahead ended at the banks of a narrow river, surrounded by trees, and cutting a winding path through the land.

The icy surface glistened and looked as smooth as glass. Snow-topped trees ran along the banks. A few branches, covered in red berries, had been caught in the ice. Craggy rocks hugged the shoreline, and a few jutted out along the river's route.

It reminded her of the idyllic rivers from postcards of the English countryside, but this haven was hidden in the mountains of Tennessee.

"The river rarely gets cold enough to freeze over, but this year it did." Peter breathed in the sweet, pine-scented air, appearing rejuvenated. "I haven't seen the ice this thick in years." He tugged her hand. "Come on."

With an exuberance she had never seen from him before, he pulled her along the path to the river shoreline.

Something rising above the water and set in the middle of the river made her stop and shade her eyes from the morning sun.

"What is that?"

Before she finished speaking, the wind changed and clouds rolled in, casting shadows across the water.

An arched garden bridge appeared in the dim light. Made of

rough-cut timber and breaching the narrow, frozen river, the quaint crossing had stone steps leading to the wooden base on each side, and a smooth, curved railing of unfinished wood. Supporting the railing were spaced crisscrosses, the knots and imperfections in the wood visible from the shore. The deck planks were rustic, uneven, and gaps could be seen, but the structure looked sturdy and idyllic in the woodland setting.

"I've never seen such a perfect setting. It's like a Christmas card."

Peter took her hand and walked her along the shore. "Lawrence and I built this bridge when we were kids."

The pain seeping into his voice touched her.

"You two did a fine job."

They reached the bridge and he broke away from her, heading down the path to the bridge. At the start of the stone steps, he tapped his fist on the roughhewn beam forming part of the railing.

She took in his guarded mannerisms, reading his apprehension in how he stared at the bridge and kept his lips pressed tightly together.

He caressed the wood. "When we were boys, Lawrence and I used to come here often. I learned how to build here. We spent days putting together forts and tearing them down when we came up with better designs."

She eased closer, following his gaze. "Does Lawrence still build things?"

"Not for a very long time."

A lump formed in her throat as she thought of her brother and the distance that had grown between them. "You two sound like

111

you were once close."

He dropped his head to his closed fist perched atop the railing. "Thick as thieves when we were young."

"And Evelyn changed all that?" Her disbelief raised her voice. "I can't believe you two can't patch things up. You are family, after all."

He shook his head and turned to her. "It's too late for us."

"I'm sure if you try, he could—"

"But you haven't tried with your family." His tone became harsh. "That's why you're here now." He paused and pulled his coat closer. "You, more than anyone, should understand some fences are beyond mending."

She wanted to argue with him, but he was right. How could Courtney encourage him back into the arms of his family when she wasn't willing to follow such advice?

Perhaps they were two misfits who would never feel at home no matter where they ended up. She'd been running from her pain just as much as Peter.

"I remember something my dad told me, right before he left. 'It's not the amount of memories that matter; it's that you have a good one to carry with you for a lifetime.'"

"Wise man." Peter nodded. "And he was right. There is one memory I have with my brother on this lake that will always be with me. No matter what happened with Evelyn, that time we had is precious."

Courtney walked up to the bridge and ran her gloved hand over the smooth wood railing. "What was it?"

He looked at her and bobbed his eyebrows playfully. She

laughed, relieved to see his somber mood retreating.

"There was one winter when the river was much like it is now. We played wild hockey on the ice."

"What's wild hockey?"

He motioned to the bank closest to them. "It's sort of like war. You must defend your bank against your opponent and not let their puck land on your side of the river. We made sticks out of branches we found along the banks, and our puck was a round pebble." He smiled and his cheeks filled with color. "We stayed out here until after dark. Our mother was livid. We were both punished for a week, but the adventure was worth it. That was the best day."

Courtney leaned over the railing and peered down at the ice. "Do you think it's thick enough to play on?"

He folded his arms and gave her a once over. "Are you willing to give it a go?"

She nodded. "I'm game if you are."

The smile that crossed his lips was the biggest she'd seen from him since that first day. The corners of his eyes crinkled, and suddenly Courtney forgot about the cold.

He eagerly scoured the bank of the river close to the bridge, looking for the perfect fallen branches. What he handed her when he returned looked more like a club that a hockey stick. The shaft was thick with a few twigs still attached, and there was no toe to push the puck along, only a slight nub at the end. The butt end where she would place her hands was bumpy and difficult to hold, but she'd make the stick work.

She noted that his stick appeared much smoother and more

like something used in regulation hockey.

Yeah, that won't give you an advantage, buddy.

She didn't want to accuse Peter of stacking the odds in his favor, but she had a feeling he was a sore loser.

With her hands tentatively in front of her, she stepped off the riverbank and onto the ice. It had been years since she'd done anything like this. She had put her competitive days behind her when she went to college, but as she got her footing on the ice, the days spent on the frozen lake at her parents' farm slowly came back.

She glided along, getting her confidence back, but then a slight bump made her lose her footing halfway across the river.

Peter was on her within seconds and caught her right before she toppled headfirst into the ice.

"You sure you're up for this?" he asked, keeping his arm around her shoulders.

She grinned, her desire for a challenge growing as she pushed him away.

Courtney glided across the surface, zigzagging and getting used to the grip of her boots on the ice.

The surface was surprisingly smooth as she sailed along. Stopping without a toe pick, however, would prove challenging.

"You're getting the hang of it," Peter called.

She tapped her stick on the ice, batting each side of the end she planned to use as the toe, finding which one worked better. She had to shift her grip a few times to find the best placement, but after a few swings, the stick felt comfortable.

"Have you done this before?"

She moved to the middle of the river and took up a defensive position. "My brother was a hockey freak. Made me practice with him every winter."

Peter pushed across the ice, appearing confident, and came up to her. "I've got a little competition, eh?"

She gave him a cocky grin. "Maybe."

He pointed to the bank behind her. "That's your side." He thumbed over his shoulder. "I'll defend this one."

A rush of adrenaline coursed through her when she found a good spot in the middle of the river. A *crunch* rose as she dug her stick into the frozen river, sending up a few chips of ice. Courtney tensed, zeroing in on Peter, ready to protect her bank.

"Out is about twenty feet on either side. Do you need me to mark it?"

She glared at him. "I can remember."

"Good." Peter removed a large round pebble from his pocket and bounced it in his hand. "First to land the puck on the opponents bank three times wins. Sound good to you?"

She crouched, taking up a defender's stance. "Prepare to die!"

Peter dropped the pebble. "Oh, this is gonna be fun."

Chapter Eleven

She couldn't feel the tip of her nose, and her cheeks had gone numb, but Courtney didn't care. The azure of the sky reflected off the ice, giving everything a surreal blue haze. The occasional fish darted beneath her, distracting from Peter's fancy footwork as he approached. She inched ahead, her boots slipping on the ice. This had been easier when she played with Matt. Perhaps her sedentary lifestyle was to blame.

She licked her lips, her eyes glued to the puck.

Peter dipped his right shoulder and pushed off with his left leg. When he bobbled and then headed right, she hesitated, and it cost her.

A rush of air brushed her face as he skirted around. He appeared nimble and confident, moving the puck like a pro.

She turned too quickly to go after him and lost her balance. The stumble cost her a second or two. Courtney pushed hard, her thighs burning as she caught up to him. Leaning on her stick, she checked his moves, battling for the puck, and applying pressure to block his chance at getting past her.

He was quick—she had not expected that. Being shorter, she had the advantage, but Peter batted at her stick and stayed in the thick of the fight. Courtney saw his tactics as a weakness. She would have dodged such interference and skated around to make the goal. When she got the puck away, she knew what to do.

She checked the distance to the shore behind her—he was getting close. She had to keep him from driving a shot at her bank, and that meant getting aggressive.

She went after his stick, fighting to get the puck, but the limbs got caught together. One of the twigs poking from her stick hooked over one from his. The jam didn't last long, they separated in an instant, but the brief lapse broke her concentration. Peter took advantage and faked a move to the left, and then he lost her when he dipped right.

He eased past her, and her anger surged. Instead of barreling toward the bank and making sure he got the shot, Peter lined up his aim and whacked at the puck.

A risky move.

The stone bounced around the shoreline, encountering a few rocks before coming to rest on a spot where the ice met the ground.

"Ha," he cried out with glee. "One point for me."

He went back to his bank, kicking across the ice with an arrogant air.

"Don't let it go to your head," she called.

"Never," he shouted.

She wiped her brow, already damp, as she made her way to the side of the river to retrieve the puck.

Her mind became a flurry of tactical moves. The opening shot gave her a lot of insight into how he played the game. He was a dangler—someone who tried to fool their opponent into making the wrong move. That was good. The tactic was something she could counteract. If Courtney moved the puck quickly and accurately across the ice, he would not have time to fake her out to steal the shot.

You got this.

Courtney dropped the puck, the dull *thunk* echoing across the river. She analyzed Peter's stance, his laser-beam focus, and then set out to meet him.

She worked the puck back and forth with her stick, getting a rhythm as she grew more accustomed to the ice. Her feet slipped less, her balance was better, and the puck was easier to control than before.

She thought of Matt as she traveled the ice, knowing he would have loved to join in.

At the halfway point in the narrow river, Peter came out to meet her, tapping his stick as he moved.

The sound was meant to distract, but her attention remained honed in on his movements. She waited for him to tell her where he planned to cut her off. When he dipped slightly to his right, she followed his lead and stayed on her left, matching him like a dancer mirroring a partner.

Peter was on her, his stick close to the ice, surging forward, appearing ready to make a steal. But Courtney was ready, and as soon as he bent slightly to his right, showing where he intended to go, she anticipated his fake and dashed in the opposite direction.

Her plan worked and Peter was caught off guard. She whisked around him, gaining speed as she charged toward the shoreline.

Courtney kept her stick close to the puck, making sure to get within feet of the shore and not make a shot that could bounce off a bump in the ice or veer out of bounds. She wanted to make this count.

The last *whoosh* of her stick as she took the shot sounded like music to her ears. The puck sailed toward the shoreline and landed right between the two large rocks she'd aimed for.

Courtney beamed, her center exploding with pride—she still had it.

"Very nice," Peter called as he came up to her side. "You're good."

She gave a curt nod. "Yes, I am."

His gravelly chuckle carried across the river. "Now who's letting it go to their head?"

He retrieved the puck and came back to her.

"Ready?" Peter bounced the puck in his hand.

Courtney admired his self-assurance and noticed how much he'd changed. He no longer carried a heaviness in his shoulders but appeared tall and proud. A radiant, lively light replaced the sadness that always clouded his eyes. He was like the man she met that first day.

Still taking in his rosy cheeks and vibrant gaze, she shifted her hips, propelling herself backward on the ice.

Courtney settled in the center of the river and crouched, gripping her stick. A trickle of sweat ran down her brow, and she wiped it away. The cold that bothered her before had been chased away by the confidence warming her insides.

The *thunk* of the pebble on the ice drew her attention. Her heart sped up as Peter came toward her with an intimidating scowl.

He plodded his way across the river, and for Courtney, his sluggish movement was a sign of his indecision. He didn't know which tactic to use against her to reach her bank. Matt had always taught her hesitation was the hallmark of opportunity.

"Take advantage of an opponent whenever you can."

She sprang into action, clamoring at him as fast as her boots could carry across the ice, the brisk breeze cooling the sweat on her brow.

By the way Peter jockeyed the puck back and forth, she could tell he hadn't expected that from her. Courtney pounced right at the perfect moment, taking the shoe of her stick and ramming it right at the puck.

The *crack* of the pebble connecting with the wood sent a vibration up her arm.

The pebble skidded between Peter's feet and careened behind him. It sailed across the ice, back toward his side of the river.

Courtney darted around him and chased the puck, proud of her steal. She had outmaneuvered him, and Peter wouldn't be able to catch up.

She pushed hard, guiding the puck and fighting the ache in her legs to get to the shore. When she drove the puck into the same two rocks as before, her victorious laugh filled the air.

She pumped her fist into the air the moment the pebble settled against the shore. She wished Matt could have seen her move. He would have been proud.

"Where did you learn to do that?" Peter bellowed from the middle of the river.

She picked up the puck while her rush of adrenaline receded.

"My brother. We spent a whole summer at an ice rink when I was nine, practicing that maneuver on each other."

Peter scratched his head, and his pensive frown returned. "Your family let a girl play hockey?"

The question roused her inner tigress. The same one that roared whenever she was considered too feminine, delicate, or dumb to compete with a man.

"Do you have a problem with a woman doing anything a man can?"

The question sounded a bit too aggressive, but Courtney didn't care. A lifetime of competing with men, from her brother to the suits in her office, had made her a pit-bull when provoked.

"No, I think it's wonderful you put yourself out there." He leaned on his stick. "The human spirit isn't limited by one's sex, only its determination."

She skated out to the center of the river to meet him. "That's very progressive of you."

Peter studied her as she came up to him. "I bet your former boyfriend wasn't so progressive."

She stopped in front of him, still holding the puck, but feeling the pain of the past weigh on her.

"Kyle? No, not at all. He thought a woman's place was in the kitchen."

"My brother was the same way." The veil of sadness returned to his eyes. "That was one of the things Evelyn disliked about him. She wanted to travel the world and see all the wonders she'd read about in books."

"And did you want to join her?"

Courtney had not meant to ask but was glad she did. She liked the person she was around him, but still knew little about his life.

Peter took the puck from her. "What do you say to making this the last point?" He raised his head to the gathering clouds. "It will be dark soon, and you need to get back to your book."

The assertive lilt of his voice told her not to press him about Evelyn. He wasn't ready.

"If I make this point, I win."

He held the puck in front of her. "And if I do, it's a tie."

She nodded to the pebble. "Then let's go."

The smack resonated across the river the moment the pebble hit the ice.

A rush of energy roared through her. Courtney jumped on the puck, wanting to get the first swing at it.

Peter outfoxed her and undercut her stick, knocking the puck to the side. He chased after it, and Courtney cursed under her breath.

She pumped her legs to get to his spot on the ice, her muscles quivered with resistance. She took in several quick breaths, fighting to stay steady. She had something to prove to herself and Peter in the last play. She could never appear weak.

He worked the puck along, sweeping it from side to side. She came up next to him, looking for her chance to steal, but Peter guarded the pebble, keeping it out of her reach, and frustrating her even more.

He kept his strokes short, and every time she followed where she expected him to go, he changed direction. Her anger took over.

The tactic she'd employed before to outplay him wasn't

working. Her mind raced with alternative measures to shut him down. An itinerary of shots she'd practiced with her brother flew through her head, and then she struck on something—an illegal trick Matt often used against her. Her lips curled into a sneaky grin as she lifted her stick, ready to strike.

She jabbed her tree branch through his legs, knocking the puck out of the way, and tripping Peter.

He hit the ice hard, allowing her to steal the pebble and work it toward his side of the shoreline.

Courtney raced along, fighting to keep her balance and never looking back. Her focus was only on winning.

She drove the puck home, the *clunk* as it hit one of the two rocks sent a thrill of victory coursing through her.

Courtney stood on the ice, catching her breath, and when she finally remembered Peter, she turned to him.

He remained in the middle of the river, sitting on the ice and holding his stick. He kept his head lowered, appearing dejected by his defeat.

"Are you all right?"

She rushed toward him; afraid she'd hurt him.

Once at his side, she knelt on the ice and inspected his pale face.

He didn't look at her. "That was cheating."

His sullen voice surprised her. "No, that was an illegal move." She sat back on her knees. "You said nothing about sticking to hockey rules."

He struggled to stand. His right boot slipped out from under him.

She went to hold his elbow, but he pushed her away.

"It was a cheap shot, Courtney."

He stormed across the ice, heading to his side of the shore.

"Aw, come on," she called behind him.

Courtney hadn't expected this. She hadn't meant to upset him, but she also didn't want to lose the game.

"I'm sorry." She remained in the center of the river, hoping he would face her. "I will let you take a penalty shot at me."

He stopped at the river's edge and picked up the puck.

For an instant, she believed he would take her up on her offer. Then he tossed the pebble in the air and using the stick as a bat, whacked the stone across the river and over her head.

She ducked and then glared at him. "What did you do that for?"

He stood, not explaining himself or offering any apology.

She ran to the opposite bank, anxious to find the pebble. She would insist they continue the game, and this time, Courtney would let him win.

He's just like Matt—a sore loser.

Using her stick, she climbed from the ice and went to the brush gathered along the shore. An acrid taste rose in her mouth. Probably guilt for pulling her sneaky attack on Peter. She hadn't considered the ramifications of her trick shot—she'd been too anxious to prove herself.

Courtney used her stick to whack at the stiff grass along the shoreline, hoping to find their puck.

"Leave it!"

She glanced up to see him standing on the opposite shore.

124

He tossed his stick aside. "We have to get back."

"I can find it. We can still play one more shot," she insisted before going back to a thatch of long weeds.

"Courtney!"

The insistence in his voice pulled her away from her search. She looked up at the sky and saw the red streaks of evening encroaching on the horizon. A heavy feeling settled in her chest and then the cold closed in. She shivered and became furious with herself for ruining their happy time together.

I'm an idiot.

Her disappointment sapped her energy. Her legs throbbed, fatigued by all the work on the ice, and she no longer felt like fighting her way across the frozen river.

She spotted the bridge and decided crossing it would be faster than fighting the ice. Courtney headed toward the arched structure, wishing she had never come with Peter to the magical place.

She stepped over clumps of brush along the shoreline, her boots sinking into thick patches of snow as she hurried to reach the bridge.

The stonework on the steps was like the mantle in the cabin. The same attention to detail reminded her of Peter. Even when he chopped wood, he had to make everything precise.

Her glove brushed the smooth surface of the wooden railing, wondering how many hours the two young men spent building the bridge. That Peter's beautiful remembrance of his life with his brother should be hidden away in the woods made her sad. If only others could see what they had done.

Then a funny indentation in the railing stopped her cold.

She rubbed the surface, not sure if the imperfection was intentional or just a play of light on the dark wood.

A portion of the railing had been expertly carved away, leaving a name raised in the wood like a bas-relief. The letters were swirled and decorative. This was professional, even, and expertly done. It wasn't the work of a lovesick schoolboy, but a man who worshipped the woman whose name he'd forever attached to the bridge—Evelyn.

Courtney's knees became weak as she traced the name she had no doubt Peter etched there. The love he'd borne for the woman became painfully clear.

Her heart grieved, sinking like an anvil in her chest. No one would carve her name into anything, or pine for her after she went off with another. She wasn't the kind of woman who lived fairy tales. She only read about them in books.

"You found it."

He was in the middle of the bridge, a few feet away. So caught up in the testament of one man's love, Courtney had not heard Peter's heavy boots or felt the bridge tremble under his weight.

"When did you do this?"

He swung his hands behind his back. "What makes you think it was me?"

She glanced at him and tipped her head. "I didn't realize how much you loved her."

The thin line was back on his lips. "Neither did she. I carved this right after she married Lawrence."

She tapped the carving with her hand. "Has she ever seen

this?"

"No. She never came here."

Courtney tried to find something to say to soothe the pain he must have felt. She could empathize. She had been through the same heartache, and no words would ever help.

She took one last look around, eager to memorize the enchanted place. Then she spotted something—a path breaking through the trees.

"Where does that lead?" She pointed at the path. "To more places like this?"

"It's not safe." He motioned for her to return to his side. "Come. We must go."

Her curiosity whetted; she didn't move. "What's wrong with checking out that trail?"

"We can't. That way is too dangerous. People have disappeared in there." He remained in the center of the bridge and stared ahead to the path. "You must never go beyond this bridge. If you got lost, no one would find you. Not even me."

The twitter of birds rose, a soft red glow overtook the river, and the wind picked up. But as she gaped at the dense trees crowding the path, the darkness appeared to close in, creating a black hole that sent a shiver through her.

"You sound like Mrs. Finn. She talked about the danger in these woods and some angry spirits who live there." She spun around to him. "Surely you don't believe in such things."

His hands balled into fists. "Don't ever compare me to Mrs. Finn."

His outburst stunned her. "I wasn't. I was just making a—"

"Unlike Mrs. Finn, I'm here to protect you." His fist came down on the bridge railing. "I wish you could see that."

He wheeled around and stormed off the bridge.

Courtney stood, dumbfounded by his reaction. His black coat flapped in the building breeze as he headed back up the snowy path that led to the cabin.

The light around her dimmed and the red in the sky became streaked with ribbons of black.

She needed to stick close to him. It would be hard to find her way back to the cabin without him.

A bitter taste flooded her mouth, and then she ran after him, afraid.

"Peter, wait!"

Chapter Twelve

Her boots skidded along the slick surface of the path ascending from the river, sending a surge of anxiety ripping through her. Once she arrived beneath the canopy of trees, the darkness became daunting. Courtney groped along the tunnel, longing to reach Peter. Occasional shards of red light would peek through the opening in the trees, giving her a brief snippet of where she was. She walked on, her steps quickening as a numbing dread spread across her limbs.

"Peter!"

Nothing.

Her glove got caught on a branch. She yanked it free and ended up losing the glove. Instead of wrestling with the branch, she trudged on.

The cold was getting worse, too. It chilled her to the core and the feeling in her fingers and toes dwindled. She shoved her ungloved hand into her jacket pocket, vowing to never leave the warmth of her cabin again.

A crush of leaves and snow came from up ahead. She gulped and charged forward.

"Peter?"

Another crashing sound, like branches moving, came from her left. She followed the noise, praying she'd found him.

More light, purple and glowing, came through the breaks in the canvas above. Then, she spotted him, darting behind a few branches, his blond hair bobbing on his head as he rushed along.

"Peter, stop."

When she reached the outcropping of branches, he wasn't there.

She stomped and moved on. Courtney wasn't sure where she was or if she was on the right path.

Peter's blond hair and the back of his coat appeared again briefly, heading to the right. She didn't call ahead but figured he'd slowed down enough for her to keep up. The grip of panic eased in her belly. At least he hadn't left her completely.

The glimmer coming through the trees darkened and soon there was barely any light to guide her. Now and then, his footfalls on the snow would give her a direction, or she would catch glimpses of his hair.

Rife with cold and distress, she started shivering. The chattering of her teeth blocked any sounds of him on the path. The blackness around her spread, and she feared she would lose all track of him.

Then, the trees around her thinned. The branches let in bits of purple light, and the tunnel widened.

She pressed on, comforted that she was out of the worst part. The clearing had to be close.

Courtney regretted the adventure. She should have refused his invitation, but what was he thinking? Who leaves a customer alone in the woods to fend for herself? What if something happened to her? Didn't he care about the legal ramifications?

"If he were my client, I would dump his butt for being an idiot."

She stepped over fallen branches in the snow, her muscles aching for rest, and her determination waning with every step.

Something rushed across an opening in the trees ahead of her. She swore she saw Peter's black coat. Courtney summoned her strength to sprint ahead and catch him. And when she pressed through a group of low-lying branches, a clearing appeared.

She stopped to catch her breath, grateful to be out of the eerie woods. But where was her cabin?

Her heart thudded, and her breath hitched in her chest as her terror of becoming lost took hold.

"Over here, Courtney."

Peter's voice came from the right.

She followed the edge of trees and then spied the smoke.

Black and billowing upward, it came from a stone chimney. She hurried ahead, and all the terror her misadventure created ebbed when she stumbled on her cabin.

She'd emerged from the woods and landed several feet away from the side of the house.

Courtney searched the clearing, and out of nowhere, Peter's black coat appeared. He was ahead of her, walking around the side of the house. His purposeful stride made her suspect he was still angry about the game.

She ran after him, pushing her tired body across the snow.

Courtney came to a halt when she saw the porch directly in

front of her. She'd expected to find Peter waiting on the steps, but there was no one there.

An unsettling twinge replaced the relief in her system.

With a tentative gait, she went to the porch and slowly climbed the steps, looking out over the clearing.

There was no sign of Peter.

"Very funny," she shouted into the woods. "You just blew any shot you had at a rematch, buddy."

Courtney waited, attentive for any sound or glimpse of him along the clearing, but all she could hear was the rustle of the wind in the trees.

She shook her head. First, he had a fit when she beat him at hockey, and then he tried to lose her in the woods. Courtney had hoped he would be different from the other men she'd known, but he was the same.

With a heavy sigh, she put her hand on the doorknob. The face of the beautiful woman carved in the front door stared back at her as if saying *I told you so.*

The moment she pushed the heavy door open something brushed against her leg. A black blur of fur dashed into the house, scaring her to death.

She walked inside and spotted the cat already on the sofa.

"Where did you come from?"

The cat stared at her with its disturbing eyes.

After the front door banged closed, she set the deadbolt and went straight to the fire.

The heat coming from the smoldering logs was heaven. Courtney removed her remaining glove and put her hands closer to the dwindling fire.

She sucked in her first relaxing breath in hours. Peter's cruel trick had exhausted her. But the game with him had been fun. She'd not been carefree with any man since her brother and his friends at the ice rink. For the first time in years, she stopped being what someone else expected and had been herself—competitive side and all.

The feeling returned to her fingers, enough for her to grip a log from the copper bin and place it on the fire. She stoked the flames, letting the heat build until the entire room glowed with orange light.

A scent drifted by—hearty, meaty, and with a light touch of sweetness.

She followed her nose to the kitchen. The red light above the oven gleamed into the darkened room.

Courtney opened the oven door and examined the contents.

The aroma of carrots, peas, and chicken in a savory pie crust sent a ripple of delight through her. Mrs. Finn must have left the shepherd's pie warming in the oven.

Courtney smiled at the woman's thoughtfulness. "I bet she wouldn't have left me in the woods alone."

Once she got the pie on the counter, she stood over it, drinking in the smell. Not waiting for her meal to cool, Courtney rustled up a plate and a fork.

She dug her fork into the gooey mess beneath the flaky pie shell. A twirl of steam rose, tempting her with the aromatic blend of garlic and onions.

She blew on her forkful of food and thought about her time

at the river with Peter. Why had he been so strange? Maybe she should apologize again for pulling her trick shot. Or perhaps he should apologize for leaving in a huff.

She leaned against the counter, holding her fork, and debated her next move, or if she should make one.

Her feelings for Peter resembled a muddied pool of water. She'd never wanted to feel anything for him. After that first day, Courtney hadn't considered him a man she'd take an interest in. But since he'd arrived at the cabin, everything had changed.

She glimpsed the chunk of chicken on her fork. Should she play it cool, or let him have it? One might drive him away and the other could scare him to death. Peter was a tough one to figure out.

Courtney was about to bring the fork to her mouth when she saw the white phone on the wall—the one connected to Peter's cell.

Why wait for him to come to you?

She put her fork down and picked up the phone.

There were no buttons to press, no old-fashioned rotary wheel. There was a crackling in the line, and then a distant ringing sound.

Seconds ticked by, and her reservations grew. Perhaps confronting him fresh after their argument wasn't the best idea.

"Peter Morris here."

He sounded upbeat. That was a good sign.

"It's Courtney."

A few seconds of silence tightened her grip on the receiver.

"Courtney. Is anything wrong?"

"Wrong? What could be wrong after you left me alone in the

woods?" She rested her shoulder against the wall. "That wasn't funny, Peter."

"I don't understand. You said you wanted to be alone in the woods. It's why you insisted on coming here."

Courtney was about to remind him of what he did but held back her curt reply. She couldn't let her anger get the better of her.

"I'm sorry. I shouldn't have attacked you like that. I just wanted to know why you ... Never mind."

A few seconds of tense silence passed before he asked, "Are you all right?"

"I guess the things I said to you are eating at me."

His lighthearted chuckle immediately brought a smile to her lips.

"Are you kidding me? I should be apologizing to you for renting you that cabin. The isolation always seems to change people. I should have warned you sooner."

She liked the softness in his voice and the musical way he spoke. He wasn't gruff or short as before, but how he was the first day she met him.

"Let's start over."

"I like the sound of that. I hope that means you're coming to Christmas dinner at the lodge."

Courtney had forgotten about the invitation. The idea appealed to her now after the time they'd spent together. He didn't feel like a stranger anymore.

"Yes, I would love to."

"Great." His enthusiasm surged through the line. "I'll pick you up Christmas morning. You will probably be hungry for some company by then."

She was about to ask him what he meant when she heard another voice in the background call his name.

"I gotta go, Courtney. Everyone is checking out today. It's been crazy. But I'll see you on Christmas."

He hung up and the line went dead.

She stared at the receiver in her hand, wondering what had just happened.

He'd never mentioned anything before about having to get back to the lodge. If he'd been busy, why had he insisted on the walk to the river and the game of hockey?

Courtney went back to her shepherd's pie, more confused than ever.

The cat's orange eyes glowed from under the tree. Startled, she put her hand over her heart. "You scared me."

The cat continued to glare.

She jammed her fork into the pie. "Why are you obsessed with that tree?"

The cat darted out from under the branches. The sleek black hair rose on its back as it ran down the hall and disappeared into the bedroom.

"That is the strangest cat."

Shepard's pie in hand, Courtney walked into the living room. She set her dinner on the coffee table, tucked the quilt around her legs, and opened her laptop.

The story on the page didn't sit well with her. The few paragraphs she read felt rushed and had no emotion. The entire book had not come together as she'd hoped.

Her thoughts drifted back to Peter. She hadn't understood the sadness in his eyes until she saw Evelyn's name carved into the bridge. Then everything had made sense. His love for his brother's wife haunted him.

She considered what she knew of Peter and what type of woman could steal his heart. Without thinking, she jotted notes on her computer, creating an outline of how she pictured Evelyn. Her face, her golden hair, her long graceful neck, and the way she moved.

Then she wrote about Peter and the heartache he kept buried beneath his rugged good looks.

Their story slowly emerged, but not the one they lived. The outline Courtney created was the story she thought they should have—their happy ending.

Chapter Thirteen

Two empty mugs sat atop the coffee table as Courtney typed, absorbed with Peter and Evelyn's love story. Her flannel pajamas had coffee stains, and her blue robe had stains as well—the result of Mrs. Finn's tortellini soup and raspberry cobbler. She knew she should get up and shower, at least change out of her pajamas, but that would only take her away from her writing.

Mrs. Finn came into the living room, wiping her hands on her apron. "It's unhealthy to not take a break, dearie. You've been working nonstop like this for almost two days."

Courtney kept her gaze on the computer as her hands flew across the keys. "I can't get this story out of my head. I need to get the whole thing down while my thoughts are fresh."

"Fresh?" She chuckled and the odd, deep sound bounced around the living room. "Your ideas might be fresh, but the rest of you isn't."

Courtney stopped typing and looked up at her. "I get the hint. Thank you."

Mrs. Finn came up to the sofa. "I wonder if you are creating this frenzy of activity because you want to remain distracted."

"Distracted from what?"

138

Mrs. Finn folded her arms and stared. She didn't speak, but Courtney didn't need her to. She knew what she was thinking.

"Working on this story has got nothing to do with Peter."

Mrs. Finn's hazel eyes went wide. "Do I look like I was born yesterday? You didn't get rattled about your story until you came back from your adventure with him."

Courtney returned her gaze to her computer. "What adventure?"

Mrs. Finn came up to her and took the laptop away and set it on the coffee table. She sat next to Courtney and put her hands in her lap.

"I may be old, but I'm not blind. You went off with him the other day for the entire afternoon. You missed your dinner. I left you a shepherd's pie in the oven, figuring you two didn't want me hanging around. You seemed happy with him. And now you're chained to this sofa in need of a bath."

Courtney rocked her head back. There was no way of getting around Mrs. Finn's uncanny radar.

"We went to the river. He wanted to show me the area."

"The river?" Mrs. Finn sounded surprised. "Never thought he would take anyone there. That's the place he goes to when he needs to think."

"He said it was special." Courtney picked at the stain on her robe, avoiding Mrs. Finn's inquisitive stare. "He even challenged me to a game of hockey. He got upset when I beat him."

"I'm sure he did." Mrs. Finn sat back. "That would upset any man. They can't be bested by a woman. Is that why he hasn't come by lately?"

Courtney shook her head. "I'm not sure. I thought he was upset with me for winning, but then when we were on the bridge, and I found the carving—"

"He showed you that?"

The way she spoke, in almost an angry growl, didn't match her diminutive demeanor. Her eyes glowed in the evening light, causing Courtney to edge away.

"He didn't show me. I found Evelyn's name when I climbed the bridge from the other side of the river. But the way he acted … He was afraid to get too close. He remained frozen in the center of the bridge. And then he turned around and went back into the forest." She hugged herself, the fear of that moment returning. "He left me. I had to find my way through the woods. I kept seeing him up ahead, but he wouldn't stop and wait. Once I made the trek back to the cabin, he was gone."

"My, my." Mrs. Finn nodded. "That sounds scary. Being lost in these woods at night is not good."

"I called him when I got back in the cabin. I wanted to ask him why he had done that to me. But he acted like everything was fine between us. No mention of hockey or the afternoon we spent together."

Mrs. Finn stood and pressed her apron with her hands. "He probably didn't want to bring up what happened. Goodness knows, he's had no love for that bridge since the accident."

"What accident?" Courtney's voice rose higher.

Mrs. Finn picked up the coffee mugs from the table. "It was a cold winter a few years back, right after his brother had married Evelyn. Peter went to the bridge a lot in those days. One afternoon,

I noticed him heading there with some tools. I thought he was going to work on the bridge. It had been several years since he and Lawrence built it." She held the mugs, a frown sobering her face. "By that evening, no one had seen him. Everyone at the lodge became frantic. We all knew how he felt about Evelyn, but we never suspected he would do something dangerous to himself."

She sighed and the sound heightened the tension in Courtney's back and neck. "You mean, he tried to kill himself?"

Mrs. Finn turned toward the kitchen.

Courtney anxiously followed.

"They found him in the river. The surface hadn't frozen over yet, but the water was still very cold." Mrs. Finn set the mugs in the sink. "He'd been carving something into the railing and fell in, hitting his head. The men who went searching for him brought him to this cabin. I was summoned to care for him. I stayed with him for three days under this very roof. He was in and out of it for a time and even called for Evelyn occasionally."

Courtney edged into the kitchen, settling against the counter as she listened to the tale.

"When he was strong enough, we got him back to the lodge, but he was very sick for a long time." Mrs. Finn pointed her finger at Courtney. "That he took you to that bridge means you're important to him, but you have to give him time. He's a troubled man. Ever since the accident, he fears crossing that bridge. He won't go to the other side at all. And who can blame him? If I took a tumble like that and almost died, I wouldn't want to set foot on that ghastly thing either."

Courtney folded her arms, digesting everything that Mrs. Finn had told her. The tale made sense and explained a lot about Peter's odd behavior.

"Why didn't he tell me any of this?"

Mrs. Finn removed her apron. "People aren't prone to giving away their secrets to strangers. I suspect he wants to get to know you more."

"Then why stay away?"

She folded the apron and set it on the counter. "Because he's afraid of getting his heart broken again."

"We're all afraid of that," Courtney insisted in a stubborn tone.

"But he's not you." Mrs. Finn gathered up her green bag. "He can't move on from the past like you. Peter has never possessed that type of strength. You know how weak men can be. Upend their fragile self-confidence, and they become lost little boys."

"Sometimes I get the impression you don't like Peter very much."

"I care for him a great deal. But I also don't want to see him hurt again. And with you, I'm afraid he will be." She stepped closer to Courtney. "You're here for a week, and after Christmas you'll go back to the city and pick up your life. Even though you tell yourself you don't want another man, you'll find one, and then you'll forget all about Peter."

A burst of anger warmed her chest. Courtney didn't appreciate Mrs. Finn's assessment.

"You don't know me very well."

"I know you, Courtney Winston." Mrs. Finn walked toward the back door. "I know your wants, fears, and what you look for in

142

a man." She yanked the door open. "And trust me when I say, Peter will never be yours."

The door slammed closed and Courtney clenched her fists.

She'd suffered a lot of indignation in the past—working at the accounting firm had given her a tough skin—but for Mrs. Finn to challenge her in such a way sent Courtney into a tailspin.

She wasn't sure if she should attribute the verbal bashing to the woman's protective instincts, or her dislike of anyone getting too close to Peter.

Not about to let the woman get the last word in, Courtney raced to the back door and wrenched it open. She stepped outside and scanned the clearing around her. There was no sign of Mrs. Finn.

Courtney studied the snowy path and headed back inside, mystified. There were no prints in the snow.

How did she vanish like that?

Courtney got an uneasy sensation that something—or someone—watched her from the shadows beneath the trees. She had the urge to run back inside and lock the door. Then something rubbed against her.

Courtney jumped.

The cat was at her feet, curling her tail around Courtney's leg.

She felt silly, but the sense of having eyes taking in her every move persisted.

She picked up the cat. "You have to stop sneaking up on me like that."

Once safely inside, she drove the deadbolt home and her edginess diminished. She still had questions for Mrs. Finn, but they could wait until she came back.

The cat tucked its head into her neck, chasing away the last of her anxiety.

"Are you hungry, sweetie?"

In the kitchen, she put the cat on the counter and opened the fridge, still simmering from Mrs. Finn's cutting remarks. Even if she wasn't the woman for Peter, that was not for his cook to decide.

She grabbed a hunk of cheese and turned back to the counter. "Silly woman was sticking her big nose into something that is—"

A *thunk* came from the dining area.

Courtney raised her head. The cat sat in the middle of the table, thumping her fluffy black tail.

She put the cheese on the counter, puzzled by the feline's behavior. Then she spotted the yellow box next to the furry creature. The other box of decorations that had been there earlier was gone.

Courtney hurried around the counter, worried about the missing box. When she entered the dining area, she found the box on the floor beneath the table, right under the cat.

"Why did you do that?" She shooed the creature off the table. "Maybe the crazy old woman is right, and I should just go home and forget about Peter and this weird place."

Courtney stooped and retrieved the box.

She lifted the lid, anxious to make sure the decorations weren't damaged.

The light from the window captured the silver balls inside and sent out sparkles onto the thick beamed walls. Entranced by the display, she caressed one of the glass ornaments.

"Meow."

The cat leaped onto the counter and stuck her nose in the cheese.

"No." She put the ball back in the box. "Don't you dare eat that. You'll puke all over the place, and I'll never let you in again."

She hurried to the kitchen to stop the cat from running off with the cheese. Courtney was almost to the counter when the cat inexplicably launched into the air and came right at her.

Shocked, she put her hands in front of her face, convinced the animal was about to attack. The cat missed and instead landed on the floor. Her balance off, Courtney went to turn, but then spotted the cat at her feet. To avoid stepping on the animal, she abruptly shifted her weight, but her momentum had the better of her, and she went tumbling to the floor.

Her hip hit the hard tile first, and then her arm. On the floor and breathing hard, Courtney cursed the cat, the cabin, and her rotten luck.

Slowly she sat up, then a sharp, stabbing pain shot up her leg.

"Ow." She grabbed her ankle, fearing the worst.

Slowly, she struggled to get off the floor by pulling herself up the counter. Humiliation burned her cheeks as she pictured Peter's delight. He would have considered her discomfort karma for her cheap shot on the ice.

She hesitated to put any weight on her ankle and opted to rest against the counter and give herself a second to recover.

An uncanny orange glint from the dining area.

The black cat was back under the tree, head hidden behind a few low branches, but its uncanny eyes stayed on her. She swore

145

there was discontent in the animal's steady stare. It radiated across the room

"Yeah, well I'm the one who got hurt. Thanks a lot."

The initial discomfort in her hip and right arm receded, but her ankle still throbbed. She put a tentative amount of weight on her left foot, and the shooting pain returned.

"Great. Now what?"

Courtney toyed with the idea of hopping into the living room to get her cell, but would she get any reception? Then she turned to the white phone on the wall but calling Peter would be the ultimate humiliation.

I'd rather suffer than have him come to my rescue.

Her stubborn pride pushed her on, and she sucked in a breath before testing her ankle again.

Much to her relief, the pain was a little less. Good news. Her ankle wasn't broken, just twisted.

All she had to do was stay off her feet for a while and everything would be fine.

Courtney hobbled to the living room, planning to put her ankle up on one of the red pillows and get back to writing.

First Peter, then Mrs. Finn, and now it seemed the cat was out to get her.

I'm gonna kill Bev for suggesting this place. Coming here was a bad idea.

Chapter Fourteen

$\mathcal{T}$he crackle of the fire accompanied the pounding of her keys as she feverishly typed. Her ankle had stopped hurting, but as Courtney sat on the sofa with her injured foot propped up on a pillow, her frustration with her situation only intensified.

She should have been working on the light modern romance the publisher wanted, but instead she continued with Peter and Evelyn's story. The narrative warmed her soul more than anything she'd written. She felt consumed, impassioned, and could not tear herself away from the star-crossed lovers. Missing her deadline was tantamount to professional suicide, but she hoped that finishing the novel would win the publisher's approval and grant her a reprieve.

It's the best thing I've ever written.

Courtney was lost in Peter and Evelyn's world—she had them living a hundred years ago in a cozy cabin in the woods and was in the middle of a tense scene where Peter confronted his brother about his love for Evelyn. The words swirled in her head as the heated emotions of both men came to life.

She barely registered when her phone vibrated under her leg. Spooked, Courtney almost tossed her computer into the floor. She didn't think the phone would work anywhere but close to the front door.

She checked the name on the screen, and apprehension sliced through her.

"Hey, Jan."

"Glad I got you, girl." Jan's usually rough voice purred with excitement. "I've been trying to reach you for days. I've called, texted, emailed, and—"

"It's the cabin. It's hard to get calls and there's no Wi-Fi." Courtney set her computer aside. "What's up?"

"The publisher called after I sent an email saying you would have the book done by the first."

Courtney rubbed her ankle, feeling her pain meds wearing off. "That's why I'm in the middle of nowhere. You insisted."

"And I'm glad I did," Jan said. "They didn't think you would have the changes done in time, but when I assured them you would, they got excited. They even hinted at a blowout promo to interest readers."

Courtney rubbed her arm, her anxiety increasing. "Jan, I should—"

"And I got them to agree to an advance." Jan's enthusiasm poured through the speaker. "It's not six figures, but it's a start. Do you know how many writers don't get decent advances, but they want to—"

Courtney's hand shook as she gripped the phone. "Jan, I need to tell you something."

"Am I not going to like this?" Jan's throaty voice rumbled through the speaker, adding to her nervousness.

Courtney repositioned on the sofa, stalling for a way to break the news. "It's about the book. Something happened after I got here. I heard this story about the guy who runs the place and the woman he loved."

"Great. Take notes and you can pitch the idea to the publisher after you get the revision for the accountant's story done."

"What if I want to write this one instead?" She cringed and hurried on. "It's a great story, and it's flowing out of me like nothing I've ever written."

"You have to finish the rewrites."

Jan's voice remained calm, but Courtney knew better. She'd seen her agent give a deadpan response to a difficult writer on the phone while throwing her coffee cup across her office.

"Have you seen the rewrites the publisher wanted?" She sat up, no longer concerned about Jan's displeasure. "They want me to change Kiera's position at the accounting firm from an executive to a secretary. What is that? Who wants to read about a secretary? I wrote a strong woman with gusto and all their notes turn her into a mouse."

"Their audience dictates the stories, not them," Jan argued. "This publisher has more numbers on their readers than you do on your clients. They have a formula for their books, and they stick to it."

"But they're changing my story, taking the heart out of it."

"That's what you have to do to get ahead in this business." A measure of irritation rose in Jan's voice. "You have to sacrifice some stories to publishers like this one to get a bigger audience. Once you have the readers, you can write whatever you want."

149

"And how can I do that when the readers will only expect the fluff the publisher has given them?"

"You can't …" A garbled mess of static poured from the speaker.

Courtney stood and hobbled to the front door, hoping to get Jan back.

"Hello. Jan, can you hear me?"

"Are you …" More garbled noise.

She held her phone in the air, checking her bars. "Jan? Jan?"

The line went dead and the *Call Failed* notice came on the screen.

She couldn't leave the conversation unfinished. She had to get her agent to see things her way, stand up for what she believed was right for her book and her career.

It took a few seconds for her to work the deadbolt on the front door.

A frigid wind blew into the cabin the moment the door opened. It almost knocked her back, but her determination to get on the porch and call Jan back propelled her outside.

Her slippers skidded on the ice coating the porch, bringing a jolt of pain to her tender ankle. She soldiered on, making sure to stay in the cabin's light, but the bars never got higher than one.

She held the phone above her head, cursing Peter and his crappy cell service.

The cold seeped through her pajamas and robe. She trembled, refusing to give up on getting back in touch with her agent.

Pushing to find the one spot where she could summon that

last bar, she stood at the porch steps and debated about heading into the snow.

Bam.

Courtney spun around. The door had slammed closed, immersing most of the porch in darkness. The only light she had poured through the front window.

She gripped the doorknob, jiggled it, but the door wouldn't budge. The icy air clung to her exposed skin as Courtney put her shoulder into the wood, kicked, and pushed, using every ounce of her strength. Still, the door wouldn't open.

Courtney stepped back, but then something about the face of the beautiful woman carved into the wood changed. She got closer, squinting into the darkness.

After hitting the flashlight on her phone, she pointed the screen at the door.

The mouth appeared different. The smile she'd seen on the door since arriving was gone. Her lips were an angry line, adding a menacing aspect to her eyes.

"What the …?"

She panned up and down the door, checking every curve, every facet, but Courtney was positive the mouth had changed. Perhaps it was a trick of the light, or her fatigue getting to her.

Courtney put the door out of her head and went to the window, sizing up how easy she could break through the glass. She peered inside, searching for anything that could help her.

The firelight swayed on the cabin walls, reflecting its orange light off the framed photos. On the sofa, nestled on a red pillow, lay the black cat, glaring at her.

"You little …"

She pushed away from the window, considering other ways to get into the home. She'd locked the back door after Mrs. Finn left. The other windows she locked from the inside earlier that evening.

Courtney went to the railing. There was no snow falling from the cloudy sky, but the cold was brutal. She wouldn't get far in her pajamas and robe.

After checking her phone—glad to see a full charge—she pulled her robe closer, fighting off a shiver. The temperature would drop quickly, and hypothermia could set in before she recognized the symptoms. Courtney had to act fast.

Perhaps away from the cabin, she could get a signal to call Peter. If that didn't work, her last resort was to break the window. If Peter had been angry before, a broken window would have him livid.

Better than freezing to death out here.

Courtney stepped off the porch and headed across the clearing to the trees. She frequently gazed back at the cabin, keeping the light of the window in her sights. The bars on her cell never climbed higher than one.

A light bobbing in the woods confounded her. She halted, thinking the phenomenon a reflection off her phone, but the brilliance coming toward her only got brighter.

Peter's warning about keeping her door locked came back with a vengeance.

She backed slowly toward the cabin, keeping her eye on the light. The closer it got, the easier to see the glow wasn't fluorescent but came from a single burning flame.

What kind of serial killer carries a candle in the woods?

"Hello?"

Her voice carried into the night, but there was no reply.

The light dipped and ebbed only to re-emerge a lot closer than before.

Footfalls came from the woods—the sound of crunching twigs and snow under a pair of boots. Her trembling worsened, a combination of the cold and her mounting terror.

Courtney turned for the porch, ready to break the glass to get back inside her cabin. In the open, she was vulnerable. Not thinking, she put all her weight on her injured ankle. A bolt of pain raced up her calf, and she toppled to the side. She caught herself on the porch railing but stumbled and fell to her knees, her blood pumped with blistering fear.

She let go of her phone and grabbed her tender ankle.

"Hey, are you all right?"

Courtney tensed at the female voice coming from the woods.

She peered into the darkness, and then the lantern appeared. It was difficult to see the person's face because of the lantern's glare. Courtney shielded her eyes, but then the stranger lowered the lamp.

She had light blonde hair that peeked out from under her red woolen hat. Her black boots crunched in the snow as she knelt next to Courtney and offered her a gloved hand.

"What are you doing out here?" She had a soft voice, one that suggested a diminutive nature. "You're not dressed for the cold."

Courtney took her hand, and the petite woman easily pulled

her to her feet. She inspected the stranger's red ski jacket and slick ski pants.

"I got locked out of my cabin."

The woman's fair-skinned face had a delicate beauty with pink and dimpled cheeks. Her small short nose complemented her smooth brow, and the lantern's glow radiated in her lively green eyes.

"I'm Lynn." She lifted the lamp to the cabin porch. "I've got the next cabin over."

Courtney limped ahead, still shaken. "I'm Courtney. I thought I had the most remote cabin here."

Lynn stayed by her side, using her lantern to light the way. "You do. I'm your closest neighbor, apparently. I've seen your lights on at night when I'm out in the woods."

Courtney stopped when a sudden giddiness came over her. "I thought I imagined that someone was watching me from the woods, but it was you."

Lynn shifted the light of her lantern toward the door. "Any idea how you got locked out?"

She gripped the porch railing and pulled herself up the steps, mindful of her ankle. "I was out here trying to get a signal on my phone, and the wind must have shut it. I can't get the blasted thing open."

Lynn stayed behind her on the steps. "Might just be jammed."

Courtney reached the top of the porch and turned, noting how Lynn seemed to almost glide as she moved, even in the bulky clothes. She'd never been as graceful in snow boots and ski attire.

"Why are you out here, Lynn?"

Lynn pointed to the sky. "I was trying to find a high point to see the stars. I love watching them at night, especially out here. There are so many. My boyfriend was with me, but we got separated. I was trying to find him when I heard you calling."

Courtney rested against the porch railing, sizing her up. "What's with the candlelit lantern? Don't you have the big fluorescent one in your cabin."

Lynn held up her lamp and shrugged. "Yes, but the shine off the modern ones block out a lot of the light from the stars. The candle is just enough to see where I'm going, but also gives me an unhindered view of the sky."

Courtney tipped her head. "Well, I appreciate you and your lantern for finding me. If you hadn't shown up, I was about to call Peter."

Lynn put her lamp down by the door. "He's great, isn't he?" She pointed to Courtney's ankle. "Do you need some help?"

"No, I'll be fine." She stood up straight, trying not to look like such a wimp. "I tripped over the cat that hangs out with me. I was told this forest is filled with them."

Lynn went to the railing and peered into the woods. "That's odd. I've never seen any cats around here."

Courtney's focus went back to the door, and then she checked the signal on her phone.

"I'd better call Peter. He probably has something to get that door open."

"We don't need him." Lynn waved off the idea. "Let's see if the two of us can get in."

Courtney hid her disapproving frown as Lynn walked up to

the door. Probably would take a bear to get the thing open, but she didn't need to tell Lynn that.

She had just pushed away from the porch when Lynn put her hand on the doorknob. Without showing the slightest strain, or even putting her shoulder into the wood, Lynn swung the door all the way open.

Courtney had tried that door, but a woman smaller than her easily pushed it open. Mrs. Finn, and now Lynn, made her feel like she should renew her gym membership.

She stared at the door as her disbelief took hold. "That thing wouldn't budge."

The light inside the cabin filtered out onto the porch. Then the living room lamps flickered for a moment, and when they calmed, they bathed Lynn in a warm yellow glow. Her clothes didn't seem as vibrant. Faded colors and small tears were noticeable on the fabric. Even the color of her pink cheeks and porcelain skin dimmed.

"This is exquisite." Lynn caressed the carving on the door. "I'd heard this was here but have never seen it."

Hungry for warmth, Courtney eased past Lynn. She stepped into the living room and the warmth embraced her. She snapped up the quilt from the sofa and flung it around her shoulders.

Lynn lingered at the open door, still mesmerized by the carving. "I'm surprised anyone was brave enough to carve the image of Perchta."

"Brave? Why is that?"

Lynn ran her fingers across the carving's face. "Because recreating the likeness of a witch was believed to be a way of summoning her spirit. It's a superstition that came over with many immigrants from Europe."

"Do you think someone carved that to summon a witch?"

Lynn shook her head. "Who knows? People often turn to the supernatural when they are in pain. Maybe they thought a witch would take away their suffering."

Courtney went to the door, and then she noticed the mouth on the carving. She ran her fingers over the pleasing smile. The intimidating snarl that had startled her before had vanished.

I swear I saw ...

"What do you know about Perchta?"

Lynn didn't cross the threshold but remained on the porch. "Not much. I remember seeing a drawing by The Brothers Grimm in one of the books where they wrote about a Frau Perchta. She is the beauty and the crone who promises punishment for those who are undeserving of love. Which, according to them, was everyone she ever met. She was also believed to have considerable powers. Some say she can drive you to your death and hold your spirit captive. She likes to collect souls."

Courtney took a wary step away from the door. "Yeah, I read the same thing in a book I found about her." She spotted the empty living room sofa. "Where did the cat go? She was here before."

Lynn rested her shoulder against the doorframe, a crease of worry on her brow. "Are you sure you're going to be all right? You seem pretty shaken."

Courtney limped to the sofa. "No, I'm good, thanks to you. Why don't you come in? I can offer you something to eat or drink. I have the best—"

"I can't stay. Perhaps another time." Lynn motioned to the laptop. "Peter spoke about you. He said you were a writer."

Courtney got comfortable beneath her quilt. "I'm surprised he mentioned me."

Lynn put her hand on the doorknob. "You should give him a chance. He's a good man and I have a feeling you two share a lot in common."

The comment stirred a funny fluttering in her belly. "You make it sound like he's interested in me."

"Just as much as you're interested in him." She slowly closed the door. "Have a Merry Christmas, Courtney."

Courtney attempted to stand and go after Lynn to thank her again, but her ankle protested. She gave up and settled back, too tired and cold to rush back outside.

She sank into the cushions, going over everything Lynn had said, especially about Peter. Sometimes strangers offered the best perspective. Courtney had suspected he liked her. Now she knew for sure.

And what are you going to do about it?

A whirr of black came barreling from the dining area, making Courtney gasp. The cat jumped onto the sofa and went to the pillow next to her. The curious creature curled into a ball, and soon the soft buzz of purring rose in the air.

The cat was just another one of the strange mysteries she associated with the cabin. The people, the woods, even the unforgiving cold, seemed off to her—like living in a surreal world where nothing made sense.

At least the fire was reassuring, and knowing another lodger was close by lessened her isolation. Her stay might not have turned out as planned, but meeting Lynn had saved her sanity. There was a rational explanation for her uncomfortable feelings, and her instincts were right—someone had been in the woods, watching her.

Chapter Fifteen

The sun streamed through a break in her bedroom curtains as Courtney lay under her blanket, fretting over her unfinished call with Jan. Where she left things with her agent had her reevaluating the path chosen for her.

The strange encounter with Lynn also dogged her. What she'd said about Peter had kept Courtney awake. The sting of Kyle remained fresh, tempering her desire to pursue Peter. Would that ever go away?

Fed up with her restlessness, Courtney tossed aside the covers and put her feet on the cold floor. The light coming into the room landed on her bedside table—the book on Perchta was gone.

"Where is it?" She flipped on the lamp by her bed. "The book was here last night."

She got up and checked under the bed. She flipped back the covers and even went to the dresser and checked the drawers.

The lamp in the room flickered, drawing her attention away from the dresser.

A *whack* came from the side of the cabin. The sound sent her scrambling to find her robe.

A thread of excitement rippled through her. At the bedroom

window, she threw back the curtains, expecting to see Peter. His two-day absence had left her disheartened. But more than that, Lynn's suggestion changed how she saw him. No longer just a nice guy she enjoyed hanging around, Courtney questioned if there could be more. Her bruised heart might not be ready to embrace another, but what would happen if she didn't take the chance? The regret of passing on the possibility of happiness would haunt her for a lifetime.

The glare of the morning sun on the snow blinded her, preventing her from seeing around the side of the house, but something told her Peter had returned.

Another thundering blow sent her to the bedroom mirror. She took a brush to her unruly thick hair, wiped the sleep from her eyes, and skipped applying a touch of mascara. Best not to appear too desperate.

In the hallway, she loosely tied her robe as the morning light embraced her. Through the window, movement caught her eye. Peter, still in his black coat and black boots, came from around the side of the house, wielding an ax. His blond hair shimmered as he strutted up to the woodpile and reached for a fresh log.

Her heartbeat quickened and she waited for him to look up and see her standing there in the hallway, but he never raised his head.

When he disappeared around the side of the cabin, she hurried into the kitchen, hopping toward the back door while favoring her angry ankle.

The deadbolt, sluggish with the cold, took a few seconds. The delay infuriated Courtney. She yanked the door open, tingling with anticipation. The frigid air was a shock to her system, but she pressed on. Her desperation to speak with Peter invigorated her more than the rays of the morning sun.

She hated being this way, but Courtney had missed the comfort of his presence. When she was with him, the problems hounding her went away. Most men created stress for Courtney, but Peter seemed to take away her troubles.

He was at the base of the steps, with a log perched atop the tree stump, ready to bring down his ax. Peter didn't look up as she stood there, not even when the blade split the log, sending kindling into the snow.

Her eagerness plummeted. She had forgiven him for leaving her in the woods, but he'd not forgiven her for beating him on the ice.

Typical.

Men boasted on their accomplishments but never wanted reminders of their failures. Women were much better at dealing with their defeats, probably since they had more of them—usually at the hands of men.

Peter collected the chopped wood and set it on top of the pile against the house. Then he went around a corner, still not looking at her.

She waited on the step, refusing to go after him, but not mad enough to head inside and get out of the cold.

When he returned, he had three more heavy logs in his arms. Peter dumped them by the stump, keeping his eyes on the wood.

"Good morning," she said, unable to stand the silent treatment any longer.

He ignored her and set one of the logs on the stump. He lifted his ax, centering the blade over the wood.

The ax came down, perfectly splitting the log in two. He worked methodically as he retrieved one of the halved pieces.

Another *thunk* cleaved the wood into smaller portions.

"Are you still mad about me beating you?"

He collected the pieces and brought them to her woodpile, keeping quiet.

She folded her arms, growing annoyed.

"I didn't do anything to you that isn't done a hundred times a day in any hockey rink across the country."

He picked up another log and set it on the stump.

The heat in her cheeks rose. "Was leaving me in those woods your way of getting even? Well then, congratulations. One cheap shot deserved another."

He lifted his ax and ran his hand up and down the handle. "I didn't leave you. I made sure you could follow me back."

"Am I supposed to be grateful to you for scaring me to death?"

He poised the ax blade above the log. "You're not dead. Not even close."

A loud crack reverberated as the ax drove into the wood.

A slither of satisfaction coiled through her when the blade got stuck halfway through the log.

With one arm, he picked up the ax and slammed the jammed log against the stump, but the stubborn log held on. Peter's cheeks reddened as he raised the ax again and kicked at the determined chunk of wood.

"You need to sharpen your ax," she said in a matter-of-fact

tone.

He finally looked up at her. "What would you know about chopping wood?"

She smirked. "I know a dull tool when I see one."

Her point made, Courtney turned back into the cabin, leaving him to stew.

But the moment she shut the door, it flew open. He stood in the doorway, the vexation in his eyes mirrored the knots in her stomach.

He put his hands on the doorframe, digging his nails into the wood. "I'm not mad about the game. I'm not a child."

She pulled her robe closer. "Then why are you acting like one?"

The harsh lines in his brow softened. "I should never have come to you. I should have stayed away and left you alone in this cabin."

Her first reaction was to balk at his confession, but then the meaning behind his words sank in, hitting her harder than any blow from his ax.

"Is that why you ran off the other day? Because you regretted knowing me?"

"I could never regret that. You have been a shining light in my very dark world." He lowered his hands and skulked in the door, a penitent line across his lips. "I'm sorry I left you. I hope you can forgive me for that and much more."

"Well, I'm sorry I made that shot."

He inched closer. "Don't be. I would have done the same."

She sucked in a deep breath, emboldened by affection. "I want you to know I could never regret anything about you. You've done something for me that I could never repay."

His half-smile crinkled the lines around his eyes. "What did I do?"

Since starting his story, Courtney had debated how much she would tell him. But standing before him, the arguments she made to protect her work fell apart. It was as much his story as hers, and perhaps knowing what she'd done would ease his pain about the love he'd lost.

She crooked her finger at him. "I have something to show you."

The fire was barely glowing when they stepped into the living room. Peter left her side and went to the hearth.

While he put another log on, she opened her laptop. Her heartfelt words appeared on the screen and a flutter of apprehension rose. What would she do if he hated the story, or worse, her for telling it? His approval meant everything at that moment. Without it, she wasn't sure she would continue.

The black cat, asleep on the quilt draped over the corner of the sofa, opened her orange eyes as the activity rose around it. When she saw Peter, she hissed.

He turned from the fire and waved at the cat. "Away with you."

The animal's scruff ruffled as it tore from the sofa and fled into the kitchen.

"You should be nicer to the poor girl."

He came toward the sofa wearing a disgruntled scowl. "Never."

165

Courtney might not have changed his mind about the cat, but she patted the sofa cushion next to her, hoping to win his blessing with her story. "Sit. I have to share something with you."

The lines around his mouth deepened. "Am I not going to like hearing this?"

Courtney avoided his gaze, second-guessing her idea. "I sure hope you do."

Her fingers hovered above the computer keys while she found the words to tell him about her book. Where to begin? There were more bad ways than good ones to approach this.

"When I came here, I told you the changes I had to make to my novel." She raised her head, anxious to keep an eye on his reaction. "The publisher wanted me to pen a story more in-line for their readers."

He sat back and folded his arms. "And I got the impression you weren't too happy about what your publisher wanted."

She arched an eyebrow. "Did I tell you that? I don't remember."

"You didn't have to tell me. I saw it in your face."

"Well, when we were at the river, and I saw Evelyn's name carved into the bridge, I realized what she meant to you and the misery it caused when she married your brother. So, I wanted to do something … to change the ending of your story."

"Change the ending?" The lines across his brow grew deeper. "I don't understand."

She clicked the mouse. "I want to read you something. Get comfortable. This may take a while."

Courtney took a breath and clenched her shaking right hand.

"'Nestled behind the snowy trees of a hidden lake deep in the forests of the Smoky Mountains, a bridge, made of wood and stone, stands as a testament to two souls. The structure is simple, like the two people whose love hewed the wooden beams and carved the stone in its foundation. Because of Evelyn, Peter built the bridge, and it was for her that he defied his family and sacrificed everything.'"

She paused, afraid to look up and see his red cheeks burning with fury. But when she finally found the courage, it wasn't anger she saw in his eyes, but tears.

"Go on," he said in a tremulous voice.

Encouraged, Courtney continued. She relaxed as he eased back, and the confidence in her voice grew as she lost herself in the story.

The cursor at the end of her document blinked, and Courtney glanced up from the blank computer page. Seconds stretched into minutes while she sat, ready to chew on her fingernails, waiting for his critique.

Peter was across the sofa from her, his gaze on the hearth, and his lips pinched together.

"You're a very good writer."

His voice had a brittle quality that sounded nothing like the gruff, undaunted tone to which she'd grown accustomed.

Courtney nervously tapped on the computer keys. "Not according to my publisher or agent. They think I have promise but a long way to go."

"You shouldn't listen to them."

"I have to listen to them if I want to get anywhere in this business." She closed her computer. "But lately I've been wondering if I want to continue."

He sat forward and folded his hands. "After what you just read to me, I don't see how you can stop. It's who you are."

His words reassured but she would need more than that to face the daunting task ahead of her.

"The stories I want to write are stories like this one. My agent and publisher want stories that will sell. Ones that fit a formula— not a very good formula in my opinion—but books that will make money."

"Didn't you just tell me a story about how I, or the character you created, went against expectations and followed his heart? You should do the same."

She closed her computer, wishing her situation was that easy. "Even though it might cost me my publishing career?"

"When you have a gift, it should be savored and enjoyed. Like those gifts placed under Christmas trees. We spend days thrilled with expectations and no matter what others tell us, we follow our hearts when it comes to dreaming about what we want. It's the same for you. Write what you want, follow your gift, and everything will work out. You'll see."

"Are you angry I used your story?"

He shook his head. "Not at all. You reminded me of the time I had with Evelyn. The happiness she brought me. To hear our story told with such love would never make me angry."

168

His approval fortified her. Where she had experienced uncertainty, she now had resolve. Courtney didn't care if going against her publisher and agent cost her a lucrative contract. Chasing the popular or bestselling formulas wasn't her style. To write with her heart was the only way she could continue. Her books had to matter.

"I'm very glad you like it. There's something about this story. I don't know how to describe it, but I want to work on this book and nothing else. My agent will have a fit and the publisher will probably turn me down, but if this is all I ever write again, the risk will be worth it."

His gaze remained fixed on the fire. "Find a way to write what you want. It's your life and it goes by so quickly. You don't want to come to the end and have regrets." He turned to her, the firelight flickering in his eyes. "I never did see you as an accountant."

She rolled her eyes. "Don't ever tell my mother that."

He wrinkled his brow as he looked her over. "Why doesn't she support your writing?"

"She does to a point. She fears I'll end up poor if I give up accounting." She set her computer aside, the struggle with her mother tensing her shoulders. "After my dad left us, she worked two jobs she hated to support me and my brother." She caressed the silver top of her computer. "When she married my stepfather, things turned around. My mother stopped working and stayed home, but in her heart, she still fears losing everything. She doesn't want that for me, but her constant hounding has strained our relationship."

"Like any parent, she wants the best for you and your brother.

What you call hounding, she calls love."

Uncomfortable, she stood and went to the fireplace, pretending to warm her hands.

"When we were young, my mother pushed us, hard. I struggled, but everything came easily to Matt. He was a better student, better at sports, and always had more friends. I always felt two steps behind him." She wiped her damp brow. "That's why I came here instead of going to my family's farm. With his new wife joining us for the holidays, I didn't want to have to compare myself to him again. He's everything my mother wants me to be."

"You don't have to compete with him. His life isn't yours." He stood and came toward her. "But I understand. I always felt that way with Lawrence."

She studied his profile, intrigued by the opportunity to talk about the woman he loved. "Is that what Evelyn was? A competition?"

He rested his elbow on the thick mantle. "In the beginning, I wanted her to see I was the better man, but she ended up seeing me—the real me. For someone to see you in that way, that's when you know it's love. They understand you, listen to you, and don't need bravado or wit or humor. They only want you."

An accounting of the men Courtney had dealt with rolled through her mind. There had been the egomaniacs who only saw themselves, the fawners who sought self-importance, the freeloaders who ceaselessly demanded, the hustlers who manipulated, and the life suckers who drained her energy and patience.

"Maybe Mrs. Finn has the right idea. I should stay away from men."

He wiped his face, hinting at his fatigue. "Her counsel is not the one you should be listening to."

"But you loved someone who shared your feelings even if she couldn't marry you. I've never come close to anything like that."

He pushed away from the mantle. "You will. Believing in love is as good as receiving it."

"Isn't that a little too simplistic in today's world?"

"Today's world is the same as any others throughout time because people are the same." He put his hands on her shoulders, his face inches from hers. "Don't become like Mrs. Finn—a woman ruled by her demons. You have a great deal to give, so stop believing you're not worthy of love, or success, or happiness. You are. Heal your wounds. Only then will you become the person you want to be."

A soothing wave of relief washed over her. The past had kept her bogged in a swampy pit of self-loathing. She dreamed of rising above her negativity, but Courtney's shaky confidence kept her tethered. Her failures reflected her lack of faith in herself. Peter was right. She had to change her insides before she could transform her life.

Her stomach rumbled. She quickly put her hand over it and giggled.

His boyish grin added a charming twinkle to his eyes. It was something she hadn't seen since their first meeting.

"I'd better do something about that. I'll make you my mother's biscuits. The best thing in the world on a cold morning." He walked out of the living room.

He seemed so upbeat that she didn't have the heart to tell him she wasn't hungry.

"Are these the biscuits you told me about? The old family recipe. I thought they were for Christmas morning."

He hesitated at the dining area, keeping his back to her. His shoulders flexed, and the air in the room became remarkably colder. She could almost see her breath. Then the chandelier in the living room blinked on and off.

What's going on?

When Peter faced her, sadness dulled his features.

"Yes, but maybe we could celebrate a little early. Just the two of us before my family monopolizes you and asks millions of questions."

The image gave her hope. "I'd like that very much."

She walked behind him, the prospect of becoming more than friends warming her toes.

Are you sure about this?

Her steps slowed as she entered the kitchen.

"Come on," Peter called while opening the pantry door. "You're going to help me."

She smiled at the eagerness in his voice. He'd been the first man in a long time to see her as she wanted to be—confident, strong, and glowing with hope just like a Christmas tree.

Chapter Sixteen

$\mathcal{F}$lour covered the surface of the black countertops and even dotted the tiled floor. The sun beamed through the dining room window, scintillating on all the dust in the air. Courtney wiped a flour-stained hand across her brow while inspecting the baking sheet of unevenly cut biscuits waiting to go into the oven. She couldn't remember the last time she had so much fun in the kitchen.

A glob of flour landed on her pajama top, exploding into a cloud.

Peter stood in front of her, displaying a mischievous grin.

She wiped away the mess. "Was that necessary?"

"Absolutely." He lifted the tray of biscuits. "You look way too clean for someone working in the kitchen."

"You're just like my brother. He loved to make a mess in the kitchen when we were kids."

He set the tray in the oven. "Why aren't you two close anymore?"

She picked up a towel, wanting to clean the counter. "It wasn't anything he did or said. He went away to medical school and didn't have time for me anymore."

Peter closed the oven door. "He's a doctor?"

She pushed the flour on the counter into a pile. "Cardiologist. Just like our dad was."

He came up to her. "You never said your father was a doctor."

Courtney dropped the towel and leaned against the counter. "Yeah, his practice was why he left. He got an offer to run the hospital close to where he spent time volunteering for a while in India. That's what my mother told us. She's never spoken much about why he left."

"And you've never heard from him in all these years?"

She shook her head, strengthening the wall around her heart. "Nope, but I'm sure my mother has. Whenever we needed money for clothes or school, checks would magically appear. Me and my brother suspected it was him, but my mother always denied it."

Peter stood in front of her, narrowing his eyes. "You ever try to track him down?"

"Didn't see the point." Courtney retrieved her towel. "He made it clear he never wanted anything to do with us."

She finished wiping the counter, meticulous about getting every particle of flour.

Courtney waited for him to say something while the constriction of her chest ratcheted higher. The suffocating feeling always surfaced whenever she spoke of her dad. Sometimes the sting of what he'd done remained as fresh as the day she'd woken up for school to find that he'd left during the night without saying goodbye.

"I had a pretty bad relationship with my father," Peter said behind her. "We could be in the same room, but it felt like we were a million miles away from each other."

She stopped but did not face him. "What did he do to you?"

"I was the second son. No matter how hard I studied, how strong I was, or enthusiastic about my chores, no matter how much I tried, I could never outshine my brother." His voice dropped, becoming almost a whisper. "After a while, I stopped trying. That's what you do when you know you can't win, you give up. But it wasn't until I met Evelyn that I changed ... well, for a little while."

Courtney slowly turned to him. "Why did you give her up?"

He scratched his head. "In my family, there were certain expectations—my brother was to take over the family assets, and I was to be given a lesser job running one of the properties. But when Evelyn came along, I was ready to give up everything. We hid what we felt for each other from everyone, including my brother. We'd sneak off to be alone—we spent a lot of time at the river—but as her wedding to Lawrence drew near, I knew I had to make a decision." He stared at his hands. "He could give her what I couldn't—a home and stability. If she had gone with me, who knows where we would have ended up? The guilt I would've felt for taking her away would have been worse than watching her walk down the aisle with my brother."

Courtney took in his rounded shoulders and downturned face. "What did she want?"

He dipped his head to the side. "A few days before the wedding, we were to meet at the bridge at the river. We were going to plan our escape. I never went."

Courtney's heart tore. "She must have been devastated."

"If she showed up." Peter went to the oven. "She could have

stayed away like me. We both knew what we had would never last."

She stepped closer to him. "But you don't know that. She could have gone to that bridge, wanting to be with you as much as you did with her. You were afraid to show her just how much she meant to you."

He slapped the counter. "No, I was protecting her. If I had taken her away, I would have been cut off from my family's money and her family would have disowned her."

Courtney's voice ticked upward. "What about love? Loving someone means never letting go."

He scowled at her. "But sometimes you have to let go. Why do you think your father left you and your brother? He was protecting you by giving you the best life you could have, even if that meant he couldn't be with you. Not all love stories have happy endings."

Her lower lip trembled. All the years she'd pestered her mother about her dad's whereabouts, she'd simply said—*he left us*. Her mother never acknowledged her pain or her brother's. But Peter had given her the answer she needed to hear.

"I never wanted to believe that. I wanted to hold on to the anger I felt for him."

He stood in front of her. "Your rage made it easier, didn't it?"

She nodded and sniffled. "When my stepfather came along, things got easier. I had a father who loved and cared for me, and what happened faded."

"But not completely." Peter lifted her chin. "You've never felt worthy of anyone's love because your father left you. But you are worthy, Courtney. Very much so."

He was inches away, his lips hovering above hers. The buttery aroma of biscuits blended with the hint of evergreen. She tipped closer, apprehension knotting her belly, longing for that first kiss.

His eyes widened the closer she got. Her heart rose in her throat, and her breathing hitched as she came right up to him and ...

Peter arched away from her. He ping-ponged his gaze around the kitchen, looking at everything except her.

She retreated, cringing at her mistake. She had pushed too hard or come on too strong, scaring Peter away.

Stupid. Stupid. Stupid.

Courtney was annoyed with herself. Every man walked away from her, eventually. What began with her dad continued in every relationship. What was wrong with her?

"I'm sorry," she whispered, dropping her head.

He took one step backward from her and then another. His withdrawal added to the burning rising in her chest.

"I should go."

His words drove the knife of her humiliation deeper. Her hands went to her burning cheeks. Years of failed relationships inundated her, burying her beneath a mound of self-recrimination.

"No, it was my fault."

He didn't stop to argue but hurried out of the kitchen.

Peter was already at the back door when she decided to run after him. She couldn't leave such an uncomfortable chasm between them. Not when they had shared so much.

Courtney sprinted to the door, an immediate need to make amends energizing her. Peter yanked the heavy door open and didn't look back before he bounded down the steps.

Her hope for forgiveness splintered. She stood on the top step, too devastated to move.

He trudged through the snow, pulling his coat around him.

She was about to call out when he reached the line of trees at the edge of the clearing.

Her gut-twisting distress escalated when he marched into the woods. He didn't bat at any low-hanging branches or hesitate as he came to the shadows. Peter simply stepped into a veil of blackness and disappeared.

The abruptness confounded her. There was no sound of movement. There should have been evidence of his traveling through the woods—tracks in the snow or traces of boot prints—but there was nothing.

The shock sent Courtney stumbling backward into the cabin. *What did I just see?*

Chapter Seventeen

$\mathcal{T}$he cold snapped her rational mind into action, urging Courtney to find a logical explanation. It had to be a trick of the light or an illusion caused by the glare from the snow. Her ragged breath and constricted chest begged her to run into the forest and make sure, but then a whirlwind of flakes rose and hovered over the spot where he had faded from view, twirling in a strange dance. The snowy vortex created a low howl, like a locomotive charging in the distance, and overwhelmed the songbirds singing in the trees.

"You all right, dearie?"

Courtney wheeled around.

Mrs. Finn, carrying her green grocery bag and wearing the same long blue dress, stood behind the steps.

Courtney had not heard her. Then again, the strange wind could have covered the sound. She turned back to where Peter had dashed into the forest. The small tornado, the weird noise, and Peter's footprints were gone. His path from the steps to the edge of the clearing had been wiped clean and the twitter of birds returned.

Mrs. Finn came around the steps.

"Did Mr. Morris stop by?" She clucked and climbed the steps. "Because you look like you just got a lump of coal in your stocking."

Courtney wanted to confide what had happened, but Peter's warnings about the older woman stopped her. "We were making biscuits, and he had to get back to the lodge."

Mrs. Finn warily eyed her pajama top. "You entertained him in your nightclothes? That's not appropriate, child."

Courtney shook her head and headed back inside. "People go shopping in pajamas nowadays."

Mrs. Finn shut the back door. "Be that as it may, it's not fitting for a woman to be alone with a man wearing such attire."

Courtney began to understand why Peter had such a low opinion of his cook.

The buttery aroma of the biscuits tempted her when she walked inside. She stopped at the oven and opened the door, wanting to hide her irritation. Mrs. Finn might have a nineteenth-century attitude, but she had been kind.

"What else went on between you two, besides the biscuits?" Mrs. Finn asked.

Courtney clenched her fists before she faced the woman.

"Nothing happened," she said in a raised voice. "Peter is a gentleman."

Mrs. Finn set her green bag on the counter with a heavy sigh. "But you wanted something to happen, didn't you?"

She spun away, about to head down the hall to change when Mrs. Finn spoke.

"Any single woman is looking for a man. It's the nature of the beast."

There was something about the woman's throaty voice that still made Courtney's skin crawl.

"My guess is that he turned you down."

Courtney waited at the entrance to the hall, questioning if she should confront the cook. After her run-in with Peter, she didn't know if she had the fortitude to listen to another of Mrs. Finn's bashings, but then again, the woman had worked for Peter for many years. She probably knew his mind better than anyone.

Her back rigid, and her arms folded, Courtney faced Mrs. Finn. "Peter has never made any advances toward me. We're friends. That's all."

Mrs. Finn clasped her hands as she took a step toward Courtney. "And that's all you shall ever be. He can never be with anyone."

"Why? Because of his guilt about Evelyn?"

Mrs. Finn gave a disinterested wave and went back to the kitchen counter. "Along with the other mistakes he's made. He's stuck where he is and can never leave."

"Stuck? You make it sound like he's trapped at this lodge."

Mrs. Finn opened her green bag. "He is. By his own doing, mind you. He chose to stay here and never leave. He could have had a better life, but he's bogged down in his heartbreak and refuses to see beyond a life outside of this place."

"He has other options. He told me about them. He never completed his masters because he prefers to stay here."

Mrs. Finn removed a head of lettuce from her bag. "That's the lie he tells himself. If he remains here, he will never be with anyone else. He can't cross the bridge on the river because of what it represents. How can you believe he will have the courage to begin again with you?"

The hostility in her voice felt like a hammer pounding into Courtney's chest. She had never experienced such contempt from anyone directly. The people she knew tended to vent their hate behind her back, afraid to confront her.

"What is up with you? Why are you against Peter and I getting together?"

She chuckled as she faced Courtney, a bold hand on her hip. "Because I know you two won't last. I know his type. The kind who are too soft to decide. Do they love or walk away? Do they feel or close themselves off? I've had much more experience with such souls, and they never choose, no matter how hard they try. And Peter will never break his bonds to the past for you. His fear holds him back." She paused and then raised her head. "Me and the rest of the staff feel he's hurt the business because of his indecision. You ask why I don't believe in love—just look at Peter and what it has done to him. I'd hate to see your fate become his, and I promise that will happen if you pursue him."

"Everyone changes," Courtney argued. "He will surprise you one day."

Mrs. Finn's cackle shook the kitchen. "Nothing surprises me. People are very predictable."

Courtney took a step back, a tug of fear rising from her belly. "I don't see it that way."

Mrs. Finn blew out a long breath and the animosity in her faded. "Spare yourself. Finish your book and go home. Leave Peter to the choices he made. Otherwise, he will end up running away and hating you as much as he hates me. That's what he does to the people who try to help him. And that's why I keep warning you to stay away."

Courtney wanted to debate her, but her argument died in her throat. Peter did have a habit of running away. He'd left her twice already when she got too close.

"I'll get those biscuits out for you." Mrs. Finn grabbed for a towel. "And I have a lovely roast to cook for your dinner. It was too small for the chef at the lodge, but the slices will make—"

"If you don't mind, Mrs. Finn, I can manage my own lunch and dinner for today." Courtney made sure to put a forceful tone in her voice. "I have a great deal of work to get through."

"Are you sure, dearie?" She flashed her toothy yellow smile. "I can be as quiet as a mouse if you need."

A sudden chill swept through the cabin. Courtney glanced back at the hearth, checking to make sure the fire still burned. The reddish glow assuaged her.

"No, please, it's fine." She walked out of the kitchen. "Take a day for yourself." Courtney turned to her. "I'm sure you have Christmas shopping to do."

Mrs. Finn set the pan of biscuits on the counter. "Yes, Christmas Eve is tomorrow, and I do have things to get."

Courtney went to the hearth and picked up the poker, wanting to chase away the cold hanging around her.

Mrs. Finn set the towel aside and gathered up her grocery bag. "You sure you don't need me?"

She stoked the fire, not bothering to look back into the

kitchen. "I've got so much writing to do that food will be the last thing on my mind."

When the back door finally closed, Courtney sank into the sofa, relieved to put some distance between her and Mrs. Finn. The woman's horrid laugh, her constant negativity, and disconcerting demeanor had worn on her nerves.

Then there was Peter. How did she begin to right the mess she'd made of their friendship? And the whole bizarre incident when he'd vanished into the trees. Why had he left her like that? She never expected him to be so childish.

Forget about him. You have other mountains to climb right now.

Her inner assertive voice was always there when things were down. It pushed her through every bad relationship, helped her secure her position at the accounting firm, gave her confidence in confronting her mother, and directed her career.

And her career needed her attention more than Peter. If she wanted to show Jan, and hopefully the publisher, that her story about Peter and Evelyn was worth the risk, she needed to finish it before she returned to Nashville. Peter's odd behavior, and everything she had discovered, would be hard to push aside, but the information could also become fodder for her story.

She settled beneath her laptop. Her fingers flew across the keys as the words consumed her once again. To get down the details of what Mrs. Finn said, and what Peter had disclosed, silenced her troubles. The world faded away, and her story became everything.

A familiar purring made Courtney stop typing and look up.

The black cat lay on a red pillow at the opposite end of the sofa, giving her comfort.

How the creature snuck around her cabin entertained her. The black queen always seemed to pop in and out at odd moments, sort of like Peter.

"Maybe it's a good thing Christmas Eve is tomorrow. The sooner I get out of here, the better."

Chapter Eighteen

Her neck ached, her back screamed for a long stretch, and her fingertips were tender. She'd spent hours on the sofa typing without a break. Courtney raised her head and the cold assaulted her.

The fire in the hearth had turned to a few red embers. The light outside the windows had faded away and only the black night greeted her.

Where had the day gone? Only an hour ago, Courtney sat down with her computer. She checked the clock in the corner of her screen and did a double-take. She had been working for almost eight hours straight.

Courtney moved her legs and grimaced when her muscles protested. She climbed to her feet, amazed to not register any discomfort. She'd heard it once said that when doing what you love, you lose all track of time. This had never happened to her while crunching numbers at work.

After tossing another log onto the embers, and making sure it caught, Courtney limped toward the kitchen, her ankle flaring up again.

The biscuits remained on the pan Mrs. Finn removed from

the oven. She took two and wolfed them down, thankful to silence her insistent stomach.

Halfway into her second biscuit, she remembered the fun she had with Peter while preparing them. He'd laughed, he'd smiled, and he'd enjoyed himself. She had, too.

The flour stain on her pajama top was still there, and when she touched it, their almost kiss brought a flush to her cheeks. But then the ringtone on her cell chased away her happy memories of their morning together.

She swiped her thumb across the screen and rolled her eyes, knowing her bad mood was about to get a whole lot worse.

"Hi, Mom."

"How are you? Are you writing? Do you miss us? I miss you. I don't want to go to my own ugly sweater party because you won't be here."

Her compiling guilt weakened her knees. Courtney didn't know where to begin.

"I'm fine, Merry Christmas, and yes, I am writing." The emotion in Courtney's voice made her take a breath before she added, "I miss you, too."

"I just wish you were here working instead of wherever you are." Her mother took a breath. "Where are you? You sounded mysterious on the phone."

She took in the fire's glow. "I'm in a cabin outside of Gatlinburg. It was the only one I could get. The cell coverage is pretty bad out here, so I might lose you."

"Gatlinburg? Well, at least you're not on the other side of the country." Laurie sighed. "Are you sure you can't come home for the Christmas Eve party?"

Courtney stayed strong. "Yes, I'm sure. I got a great idea for a new book, and I've been working away."

"I thought you had a deadline."

Courtney put her feet on the coffee table and sat back. "Yeah, well what the publisher wants and what I want are two different things. Anyway, I found something better to write about. It's a story I really believe in."

"Then you need to write that one instead."

The comment was very unlike her mother. She never supported bucking the system.

"I thought you would want me to do what the publisher wanted. You never cared for anything I wrote before."

"Oh, please, Court. You know I care. I read your last two books, and I was proud of what you did. Gerald bought several copies to give away at our Christmas party. Why don't you come home and autograph them? You can stay until—"

The lump in her throat became hard to ignore. "Mom. I need to get this done. You know if I come back to the farm, you'll have an endless list of things for me to do."

"It's because I need your help. You always help me during the holidays. I feel lost without you."

She slumped. "What about Missy?"

Her mother's loud sigh made her grin. "She's a sweet girl, but she has no idea how to hang garland on a tree, and her cooking skills leave a lot to be desired. Your brother will waste away while she tries to figure out which burner to use."

Courtney laughed. "She's nice. Give her time."

"Your father likes her."

The way she said *father* awakened that old pain in Courtney's heart. "He's not my father. Gerald is my stepfather."

"But he thinks of you as his daughter." Her mother's voice turned colder. "Why do you insist on bringing him up, especially around the holidays? Gerald has worked hard for you and your brother. He's given you his name. What else must he do to prove you are his?"

Her grip tightened on the phone. "Maybe if I knew what happened to my dad, I could accept Gerald. It was easier for Matt. He doesn't remember Dad, but I do."

The silence on the phone lingered, and Courtney fumed. Her mother's silence usually signaled the topic of conversation had come to an end.

"What brought this on?" Laurie asked.

"Just because I don't mention him doesn't mean—"

"Courtney, you only bring up your father when you're upset." Her mother put a soothing lilt in her voice. "I even remember back when you had a bad day at school, you asked about him. This isn't about Kyle, is it? I thought you said—"

"It's not Kyle. Well, maybe a part of it is. It's just that …" She rocked her head back against the sofa, searching for words. "Every time I look in the mirror, I see my dad. You always said I take after him. And the older I get, the more I wonder if I'm like him. I can't keep a relationship, and I'm not making any headway at what I want to do. Here I am, offered a great opportunity with this publisher, and what do I do? I start writing another book." She sniffled and wiped her nose on her sleeve.

"Maybe you're writing a new book because your heart wasn't in the old one. Which makes you very much like your father. He had to follow his heart in everything he did."

Bitter anger tightened Courtney's throat. "So, he followed his heart and left his children?"

"No, that wasn't why he left. You were too young to remember how unhappy he was and how unhappy he made us in the process. He was a brilliant surgeon, and everyone who worked with him respected him, but they didn't have to live with him."

"He left because he was unhappy with us?"

"No, because his heart was in India," her mother said. "He wanted to go back and help the people there, and after trying for years to make him happy here, I knew I had to let him go."

She bit her lower lip and grabbed the corners of the quilt over her legs.

"Is that where he is?" She fought to keep her voice steady. "Matt and I always suspected you kept in touch with him but never wanted to tell us."

Courtney waited with her breath suspended in her chest. She didn't know why this time would be any different from the thousand others she'd asked, but she hoped perhaps her mother's defenses would give way.

"Why is this important to you?" Laurie asked softly.

"Because when I look in the mirror, I see him." Tears welled in her eyes. "When I was little, I used to cry myself to sleep, afraid you would get mad at me for looking like him."

Her mother's heavy sigh stilled her tears. "You never told me that."

"You were working two jobs, trying to pay the bills. You didn't need to hear any of it. I kept a lot of stuff from you then."

"That was never what I intended." Her mother's voice faded slightly. "Before your father left, we discussed what would be best for you and your brother. He wanted to prepare you both, but I wanted a clean break. After he was gone, you and your brother were devastated, and I didn't have the strength to tell you the truth about what happened. I figured it would be better to never speak about your father and move on. Then Gerald came along, and we became a family. I didn't think what happened with your father mattered. I knew Matt had gotten over him, and I hoped you had, too."

Courtney clung to her mother's every word, with years of questions straining for an answer.

"Your father first told me about the job offer in India after your brother turned two. I had listened to his stories about the poverty and disease, and I knew I could never subject you and your brother to that. Your father agreed and also worried about our safety. We wanted the best for you, and he decided to go on without us. After he left, I got angry. How could he choose others over his own family? I filed for divorce and refused to let him speak to you. In time he stopped calling, stopped sending letters."

"You?" Courtney spat out. "You kept him from us?"

"He was never coming back. I wanted to make sure you and your brother put him behind you."

Courtney sat up, infused with hope. "Do you know where he is now?"

Her mother's long pause was followed by a heavy sigh.

"He died while tending to patients in a cholera outbreak in the village where he lived."

Everything slowed, and the living room became a dizzying whirlwind. She balled the quilt in her arms, fighting the emptiness that threatened to swallow her. She tucked her legs and dropped to her side on the sofa, the phone against her ear.

He's dead.

The words rang over and over in her head. Years of dreaming about his return and sweeping her into his arms evaporated.

"The authorities there told me he'd remarried, but had no children," her mother said, her voice sounding distant. "I tried to find a way to tell you and Matt. But you were fighting for your promotion and Matt had just proposed to Missy … I didn't have the heart."

"He was my dad," she whispered. "You should have told me."

"He made a commitment to me and this family, but he didn't see it through. And you are nothing like him. You don't run from your commitments. You never have, and you're not about to now."

Courtney wiped away the tears on her cheeks. "I don't understand. What does that—"

"You went to that cabin to write a book you didn't believe in because you thought it was what everyone wanted. You discovered you need to write what you want. No amount of success is going to make up for doing what isn't in your heart."

"But my life could have been different If I'd known him better." She sat up, shaking all over. "Maybe I wouldn't have wanted men I could never have and—"

"Courtney, the only person you need to love you is you."

The strength coming from her mother's voice dried her tears and eased her trembling.

"As soon as you start doing that, you will find someone else who loves you, too."

She wanted to yell, hit something, grumble that her whole screwed up life was the result of lies and deception, but Courtney kept a lid on her emotions.

"I have to go, Mom."

"I understand. But if you want to talk, I'm here for you."

Courtney dropped her phone on the sofa. Her isolation became suffocating.

The cat opened its eyes and watched her as if anticipating an outburst.

Filled with nervous energy, Courtney paced, stomping in front of the fireplace.

A barrage of questions came and went. The more she brooded, the worse the suffocating sensation in her chest became. Soon the living room didn't have enough air. The walls closed in and she had to get out.

Courtney went to the dining area, headed for the back door, and sucked in deep breaths. The vise around her chest choked off her will. Courtney bent over, grabbed her knees, and battled to regain control of her emotions.

Something soft brushed against her leg. The cat instinctively knew she needed help.

Courtney swept the furry creature into her arms. Its soft purring eased her ravaged emotions, chipping away at her panic until the intensity became manageable.

There were many things she should have said to her mother, arguments she should've started, but each scenario left her more disappointed in herself. In her heart, she had known why her dad never contacted them. Courtney just didn't want to accept that the mother she had adored could have been callous and cruel.

The cat fidgeted in her arms and she set her on the dining table next to the boxes of decorations. She remembered all the Christmases her mother had worked hard to make special. The hours spent painting ornaments, the hot chocolate, the parties, the forced cheer. It had all been a lie.

Courtney lifted the cover on one of the boxes.

"To not decorate the tree and welcome the spirits to the celebration would incur their wrath. They would send the Yule Cat to seek vengeance."

Peter's childish story brought a wave of acid into her mouth.

He had let her hope something could exist between them. Her mother let her cling to the belief her dad would return when she knew he would never come home. Even Kyle had lied. He had made her foster the fantasy of their having a long life together, but he never intended to marry her.

The boxes on the table represented a season that was nothing more than a commercialized reason to deplete savings. How pathetic was that?

Disgust permeated her bones as she flung the box top away. After rifling through the shiny balls, she discovered something sharp buried in the mass of silver—an eight-pointed star of

Bethlehem. Most of the gold and silver glitter had worn away, but the sad little ornament still glistened in the kitchen light. The memory of that last Christmas with her dad brought all her heartache to a fiery crescendo.

Every lie in her life came down to that star. How much hurt and desperation had she wrapped up in a pretty red bow and buried under a Christmas tree over the years?

She squeezed, crushing the center of the star, caving in the sharp points and taking immense pleasure in destroying what the ornament represented—a childhood fantasy. The crunch of the plastic invigorated her. She rolled her hands, making sure to leave nothing but dismembered pieces. Satisfied, she dropped the decimated decoration on the dining table with a sneer.

She picked up one of the shiny silver balls and held it in front of her. The dark color of her hair and eyes shone in the reflection. Her dad stared back at her.

Rage flowed through her. She threw the glass ball across the room. The sound of glass breaking made Courtney feel like she could do something to show the world how fed up she was with being trapped in her miserable existence.

She selected another ball and sent it hurtling into the wall. The shards settled in the same place as the first ball, creating a mess of scintillating glass.

In a frenzy fed by all her pent-up anguish, Courtney went through the box. She flung each ornament as hard as she could. Tears blurred her vision, and the pop of glass shattering echoed throughout the house. When there were no more balls to destroy, she took the garland and ripped it apart. Courtney tossed the remains into the air like confetti, delighting in the way it landed at her feet, a shredded mess.

She opened the second box, eager for more. Christmas lights made of small bulbs on green wire lay in a knotted mess. Unscrewing the bulbs would take too much time, so Courtney removed the curled cords and whacked their multicolored lights against the table, sending up splinters of glass.

When her frustration and sadness had ebbed and there was nothing left to destroy, she stopped and inspected her hands.

Glitter and specks of colored glass covered her skin. More dotted her shirtsleeves, along with scraps of silver garland. The colors might have hypnotized, but the anger she'd wanted to release was still there, bubbling beneath the surface, a stubborn ember refusing to be extinguished.

Numb and sniffling, she sank to the floor, accompanied by the crunch of the glass under her feet.

She sat with her chin tucked against her chest for the longest time, wallowing in the dull throb of her loss. All the things she could have been, the happiness she could have lived, passed before her eyes, deepening her pain. Was that what hitting rock bottom felt like, or would things only get worse?

A light swish came in front of her as if answering her question. She raised her head and sitting in front of her, in her usual place under the tree, was the black cat.

She stared with her funny eyes as if saying, "I understand completely."

Perhaps it was her fatigue or the fact that there were no more ornaments to destroy, but somehow seeing the cat beneath the tree brought Courtney out of her lethargy.

She slowly reached for the table to pull herself up, reprimanding the time she'd wasted feeling sorry for herself. It was time to tuck the past into the empty spaces of her heart and get back to the only thing that mattered—her writing.

Chapter Nineteen

*T*he aroma of bitter coffee rose from her mug as the heat from the restoked fire chased away the chill. Courtney stood before the living room window, collecting her thoughts for another day of writing. Her gaze kept returning to the mess in the dining area. She pictured Mrs. Finn's astonished face when she walked into the cabin. She would make amends by cleaning up the broken glass and shredded garland and would reimburse Peter for the costs. But for now, the shambles kept her from tumbling deeper into her depression.

Snow had fallen during the night, adding to the drifts outside. She considered if Mrs. Finn would trek her way through such conditions. The quiet in the cabin made her miss the older woman's dour predilections. Then again, it was Christmas Eve. All the lodge employees might have the day off.

Courtney opened her laptop, anxious to get more work done on Peter and Evelyn's story. She settled on the sofa, and let her fingers hover over the keys, waiting for inspiration. But as soon as she got an idea of where to go with the plot, her focus would drift to her mother, or Peter, or her dad, compounding her doldrums.

"Meow."

The cat jumped off the sofa and headed for the kitchen.

She put her computer aside. "What is it?"

She got up and walked into the kitchen in time to see the cat trotting toward the back door.

Courtney flipped on the light in the laundry room. The cat stood on its hind legs, scratching at the wood.

"You need to go out?" Courtney went to the back door. "All right just give me—"

A slight thump from the other side sent her heartbeat racing. *He's come back.*

She frantically worked the stiff deadbolt.

She could apologize and invite him to stay, or even take up his invitation to return to the lodge—anything to avoid the loneliness hounding her.

Courtney finally got the bolt drawn back and cracked the door.

The cat took advantage and bolted outside.

She silently cursed the animal's escape and hurried to the back step, more anxious to see Peter than follow the cat.

A gentle breeze pushed the tops off the snowdrifts, sending waves of flakes across the clearing. More piles abutted the trees and big rocks lined the outskirts of the woods. The fresh snow would make the journey treacherous for anyone coming to the cabin. It would explain why she hadn't seen Mrs. Finn. But what about Peter?

She climbed down to the second step, stretching to get a look around the side of the cabin. The woodpile sat abandoned with a fresh dusting of snow. No boot prints led to or from the house. She peered into the white landscape, hoping for a hint of Peter's black coat.

Her excitement fizzled. Where had the noise come from?

The cat trotted across the fresh snow, holding her tail high in the air.

"Sweetie, don't go far," she shouted, knowing the cat wouldn't understand her.

Courtney hurried to the bottom step where the snow met the wood. Large cat prints headed out into the snow. They struck her as bigger than any she'd ever seen—more like a predator than a domestic cat. She followed them across the clearing to the trees.

They ended in front of the cat. She sat, not moving a muscle, next to a snowbank. Her eyes seemed more intense against the bleak panorama.

The animal's orange orbs took on that creepy glow. The unnatural light permeated the surroundings, saturating everything with the unusual hue.

Almost instantly, the light breeze died. Snowflakes fell to the ground, and swaying treetops came to a standstill. An unnerving silence overtook the clearing. Even the birds went quiet.

Her gaze returned to the cat. It remained across the clearing from her, its otherworldly stare focused on her.

Thump.

Her hand flew to her chest.

The sound came from the side of the cabin.

There has got to be someone here.

Courtney stepped onto the snow, eager to find the cause. The drift covered her ankles and roused a horrible shiver. She trudged around to the woodpile while the wet snow seeped through her pants legs.

A little out of breath, she arrived to find Peter's ax was where he'd left it, lodged into the stump. Snow dusted the handle, but there was no sign of him.

The knot in her belly constricted.

A stiff breeze brushed past and flurries of snow danced along the ground. The birds struck up with song again, and the rustling of the trees returned.

Courtney rubbed her arms, wishing she'd stopped to get her jacket.

Dark clouds gathered, covering the sun's rays and sending shadows across the ground. A tingling sensation rose in her arms as if an electric charge hung in the air. The building breeze rocked the tops of the trees, and a funny hissing, like an angry snake, rose from the woods.

There would be no snakes out in the winter. This was something else.

She spun around while that odd feeling overtook her. She wasn't alone. Her inner alarm bells went off. There was something or someone out in the woods, watching her.

She glanced back at the cat, which remained at the edge of the clearing.

Courtney patted her thigh. "Come on, buddy. Let's go back to the fire."

But the animal didn't move. It only glared at her.

A prickly dread spread over her limbs. Something wasn't right. The wind grew stronger, bending the tops of the trees, the air became bitterly cold. The cat never yielded to the blustery breeze, and never took her eyes off Courtney.

"Cat, come here!"

The feline rose to its feet, but instead of coming to her, the creature turned and leaped behind a tree.

A wave of disbelief weakened her knees. Was everyone going to leave her?

The woods around her closed in and the air became thin. She didn't want to go back inside and be alone. The cat had been her only companion.

Courtney plodded through the snow, edging closer to the line of trees. What if something happened to the sweet furball? She had lived in the woods before her arrival and would return there once Courtney left, but after their time together, she couldn't just abandon her. What if the animal felt lost and alone after believing she had found a home?

"Cat?" she called. "Come back."

A horrid screech, like an animal being torn apart, came from the direction where the cat had disappeared.

Courtney went rigid, a sickening wave of terror rising in her chest.

"Cat!"

She attempted to run, but the weight of the snow made it impossible. She plowed toward the trees, swinging her arms with everything she had.

The low-hanging branches snuffed out the dim light of day. She stumbled, trying to remember the way Peter had taken when they'd gone to the river, but she wasn't on any path she recognized.

She found the cat's prints, leading deeper into the woods. Courtney debated following them. If she got lost, she could always use them to find her way back.

The desperate cry of an animal, in pain and afraid, filled her ears.

"Oh my god."

Images of her injured fluffy companion spurred her on. Courtney ran over roots in her path and jumped over the occasional rock, blocking her way. The trees closed in, and the snow turned to mud.

Courtney had to take her time through the terrain. She kept an eye out for the cat, stooping to peer behind thick clumps of bushes or high banks of snow. The cold became more severe the deeper she moved into the woods. The silence also bothered her. The birds and animals she'd seen while out with Peter had vanished, making the woods feel like a ghost land.

Courtney questioned why she was out in such horrid conditions. The fur-covered cat was suited for the cold; she wasn't. She stopped. Small prints on the ground begged her to go on, but the darkness ahead worried her.

She peered through the trees behind her, attempting to spot the cabin. The thick log walls appeared through breaks in the branches, and the tight knot in her chest eased.

Courtney followed the pawprints, brimming with confidence. *Once I get her back inside, I'm never letting her out again.*

A fallen tree popped up in her path. She didn't remember seeing anything like that before with Peter.

The cat's prints were on the snow that covered the downed

tree trunk. She reached out to touch the large indentations. She was so intent on the tracks that Courtney didn't notice when something came barreling out of the trees.

A violent wind almost knocked her to the ground. Courtney covered her eyes while snow, leaves, and light twigs thrashed about. She dug her heels into the mucky ground and was about to reach for a tree to hold on to when the wind suddenly ceased.

Shocked by the ferocity, and how quickly the gale died away, she looked around. The eerie quiet made her wish she had stayed in the city.

There is something seriously wrong with this place.

She brushed the leaves and snow from her hair and face, but when she glanced down, the air left her lungs in one sharp gasp.

The cat's prints on the downed trunk had been wiped away. She searched the snow, but there wasn't a print left.

Fear almost bent her over.

Courtney batted aside branches to get a peek at the cabin.

All she could see between the trees was tall, white piles of snow. The log home was gone.

Panic seared through her every muscle, taking away her strength, but imploring her to run.

I must go back.

She set out, following the same path she'd taken, checking the landmarks she'd passed heading into the forest. With every step, her feeling of helplessness escalated.

The house should have been just ahead. She hadn't gone that deep into the woods and was sure she was heading in the right direction.

Courtney smacked branches out of the way, anxious to see ahead, but every branch she moved, the same scene greeted her—mounds of white snow.

This can't be happening.

Her hand went to her back pocket looking for her phone, but her lifeline to the outside world wasn't there. She remembered setting it aside on the kitchen counter.

Calm down. It's fine. You can do this without your phone.

But the voice in her head could not silence the fear swelling in her heart—she was lost.

Rustling rose behind her. She relaxed, believing she'd found the cat.

"Finally ..."

She turned. Nothing was behind her. The rustling started again, but this time the sound came from the side.

She stood, unable to move or even breathe. Wasn't this what predators did? She remembered the scene from *Jurassic Park* with the velociraptors. Should she remain still or run?

But this isn't a movie. Think.

A low, deep growl came from the woods ahead.

Her knees buckled. Her breath came in short gasps, and she clasped her hand over her mouth.

The branches next to Courtney shook, sending clumps of snow plopping on the ground.

She couldn't move or breathe. Her terror had rendered her an easy target.

A low, fiendish growl came from the shaking branches next to her. Courtney covered her mouth, cutting off a scream.

She didn't wait to see what came after her. Courtney hopped over a few fallen branches and ran as fast as she could.

Her feet slipped as she maneuvered over stones and debris, fighting to get away from whatever undoubtedly pursued her. The sound of her gasping breath and galloping heart made it impossible to pick up any movement behind her.

She kept going, never looking back. Looking back was a big no-no in the movies. Twigs snapped against her face and scratched her hands. She didn't register the pain, only the panic begging her to not stop running until she reached the cabin.

Out of breath, her muscles screaming for a rest, she stepped around a tree and pressed her back against it. When she had finally stopped gulping in air, she found the courage to check around the other side of the trunk, terrified.

Her footprints were haphazard and wobbly as if she staggered the last few paces to the tree. She scanned the shadows, scoured the gaps between the branches, and squinted into the tight bunches of trees, attuned to every sound around her.

Nothing.

There was no bear, no large creature gnashing its teeth. The only thing she saw was snow, woods, and darkness.

She sagged against the tree, but as she looked around, her relief retreated. She had no idea where she was. There was nothing familiar from her other journeys into the woods. Without the cabin to guide her, she had no idea which way to go.

Courtney raised her head to the sky, remembering what Peter had shown her.

The sun, what she could see of it, appeared to be in the eleven o'clock position. She stretched out her left arm and pointed her hand toward the sun.

"That is east." She stuck out her right hand in the opposite direction. "West. Then I'm facing south, and my back is to the north … I hope."

"Head south anywhere on this land and you will either run into a road or the lodge."

The memory of his deep voice gave her confidence.

Courtney set out, following the narrow opening in the trees ahead of her.

Note to self—never rent a cabin in the woods again.

Chapter Twenty

$\mathcal{A}$ hammering pain in her legs forced her to stop for a rest. She'd lost the feeling in her fingers and toes a while ago, and the loud rumbling of her belly had replaced her panic. Courtney's emotions had dulled, and her mind had zeroed in on one goal—finding the lodge or the main road.

In this part of the forest, she'd seen signs of life. A red fox, its fur thick for winter, darted across her path. Cardinals flitted about, and one determined woodpecker banged on a tree trunk as she walked past. The growling had not followed her. Courtney was thankful for that.

The path she traveled was strewn with rocks, leaves, and fallen branches, but everything looked the same. One tree was just like another, one rock had the same markings as several she'd seen. She hoped she wasn't heading in circles and kept stopping to check her position against the sun, but Courtney feared she might have ended up deeper in the woods than coming out of them.

The light was against her, too. She kept an eye on the sun, dipping lower in the sky. With the red fingers of evening stretching over the tress, she guessed she had maybe an hour before she became engulfed in darkness.

"Don't react with emotion when things get tough. Use your head and find a solution."

Her stepfather's voice chased away her jitters. She took a breath and embraced his wisdom.

Gerald taught her to approach every situation with calm. A soothing influence, Gerald had always kept her grounded. Courtney prayed she would get to see him again and tell him how sorry she was that she'd never embraced him as a father. She'd held on to the myth of her dad coming home, and in the process, kept Gerald at arm's length.

She wished her brother was with her. Matt always turned every disaster into a comedy. What she would give to hug him once more and tell him how much he meant to her.

And what will you tell your mother if you see her again?

She slapped branches out of the way. Her anger combined with a longing to see the infuriating woman once more. She was sure forgiveness would come one day after lots of shouting and tears.

With the last dregs of eerie pink light coming through the trees, she struggled to make out the path ahead.

She wiped the dampness from her face when she spotted a clearing behind a thicket to her right. She must have come to the end of the woods and possibly the end of Peter's property. The road to the main lodge would be close, and she would finally be out of danger.

It was the first glimmer of hope that had roused in her since heading after the cat.

Courtney forged ahead, tripping over a log and nearly

toppling over. Her shivering made walking difficult. She pictured a warm fire, asserting mind over matter to get her strength back.

The fatigue in her limbs evaporated as a rush of adrenaline helped her run to the edge of the clearing.

With the last few low-lying branches pushed aside, she stepped onto the fresh layer of snow on the cleared land.

Her excitement drained out of her faster than water from a bathtub.

Ahead of her lay a circle of land, clear of any trees and brush, covered with snow. The evening light filtered through the clearing, allowing her to make out how the ground gradually climbed to a small hill.

The wind dashed, stirring up the snow. No birds dotted the surrounding trees, no wildlife foraged about. All the animals she'd seen had disappeared.

"No, no, no!"

Courtney wanted to cry, to scream, but instead, she pushed aside her panic and collected her thoughts. She had to be smart if she wanted to live.

Perhaps she'd gone farther than Peter's land. She looked up at the edge of the sun dipping below the sky, rethinking if she wanted to head back into the woods in the dark. What choice did she have? But first, she needed to get her bearings.

Courtney climbed the rise and stood at the crest on the hill. She was level with the treetops; unfortunately, all there was in every direction were more trees and dense foliage. She couldn't find any cabins, chimney smoke, roads, or even the outline of the river Peter took her to.

The breeze picked up and cut through her, resurrecting her shivering. Warm thoughts of fire or hot cocoa failed miserably to stem the quaking in her muscles. Courtney had to find shelter soon, or she might not make it out of the woods alive.

Stay calm. Keep moving.

She proceeded down the hill, debating which way to go. There was no hint of civilization in any direction.

After lining up with the setting sun, Courtney checked her position. She faced south and held her breath.

"Okay. Keep going."

She put her hand out to push a few branches aside when footsteps crunching in the snow came up behind her.

Anticipation tingled through her like electrical sparks, taking away any hint of the cold. Courtney turned to the hill and squinted in the fading light, looking for her rescuer.

She was about to call out when a low, menacing growl filled the air.

Her mouth went dry and her stomach dropped to her knees.

Oh, God!

The outline of a creature, larger than a dog and covered with a thick fur, crouched while slinking down the hill. Powerful muscles flexed beneath its coat while keeping its pointed head low to the ground. Broad shoulders rolled from side to side, showing off the animal's grace and predatory prowess.

Courtney's entire body shook. She was too afraid to move, too afraid to draw a breath.

The creature pulled back the lips on its long snout and showed sharp white fangs. It glared directly at Courtney. Its round, orange eyes shone like ominous beacons through the blackness engulfing the hill.

Courtney fell backward, her legs giving out. Adrenaline pumped through her muscles, accelerating her heart, and forcing her to gulp in deep breaths of cold air.

She scurried to her feet while her eyes remained glued on the hideous creature. She took a tentative step back, feeling the path behind her, making sure it was clear. If she wanted to survive, her only chance was to make a run for it. The woods, filled with trees and uneven paths, gave her a better chance than facing it in the open.

Thanks to the *Discovery Chanel,* she knew running from wild animals was a bad idea, but backing slowly out of the woods was hardly an option. What other choice did she have?

Courtney tensed, readying her body while her mind raced with a million things that could go wrong.

The hulking animal was only feet away, pausing and crouching as if ready to strike.

Do it. Run.

The words stormed through her like a gunshot signaling the start of a race.

She darted through the gap in the trees behind her. Her feet sank into the snow. Fright gave her energy as she tore through the woods.

Soon darkness surrounded her. The canopy of trees blocked out any trace of light.

She could barely make out what was ahead. She smacked away branches and tripped over stones, but Courtney didn't stop. The bitter taste of panic, the sweat trickling down her temples, and the burn of her lungs drove her deeper into the woods, desperate for an escape.

Courtney wanted to scream for help, but her parched throat was too raw to utter a sound.

She slowed, and when she came to rest beside a thick trunk, Courtney stopped, gasping for breath and retching. Her muscles quivered with fatigue as she bent over, gripping her knees.

When she could stand, she listened for the animal coming after her, but she only heard the wind cutting through the trees. Wrapping her arms around herself, the tears came.

Courtney tried to calm down, believing this was not her end. She could still push on and find a way out of the maze of trees, but as she sank to the cold ground, doubts about her survival overwhelmed her.

Then, something shone in the darkness—a bouncing yellow light.

A speck at first, the orb quickly grew, shooting out long rays through the gaps in the trees.

She wiped her face, questioning if her mind was playing tricks. She'd read about people in dire circumstances seeing strange lights. Perhaps that was happening to her.

"Courtney!"

She gasped and the sound echoed across the woods. Her hard, quick pulse was in her throat.

"Peter!" she yelled, sounding hoarse, and got to her feet.

The light came at her quickly. The rays radiated outward, illuminating a lantern powered by a single candle.

His footfalls crashed toward her. She'd never heard such a wonderful sound.

In an instant, he was next to her. His lantern plopped to the ground, and she caught a glimpse of the mud covering her jeans and shoes.

His strong arms went around her waist, and he held her for a moment. The warmth of him energized her depleted body. He wasn't a mirage. He was real, and he had saved her.

She melted against him. The pounding of her heart eased and the burn of acid in her throat evaporated.

"I've got you. Now tell me what happened." His deep smoky voice was in her ear, reassuring.

She leaned into him, thankful for his strength. "I opened the cabin door and the cat ran into the woods. The next thing I knew, I got lost and then something chased me. I heard a growl and I ran. I had no idea how to get back to the cabin. I ended up on a hill, and then this black snarling thing came at me. It had hideous eyes and sharp teeth."

"I told you never to go far from the cabin. It's dangerous out here alone. What were you thinking?"

His harsh tone sent a jolt of shame through her. She pushed away from him, feeling like a child being reprimanded.

"I wanted to find the cat." She held on to the tree next to her while she stood. "She's been the only friend I could count on since arriving here."

He drew closer. "I'm still your friend."

She took a step back, still shaken. After her encounter with the snarling animal and spending the day lost in the woods, the last thing she wanted was to antagonize the man who had rescued her.

"What are you doing out here?"

He removed his black coat and slipped it around her shoulders. "I went to the cabin and found the back door open. I've been looking for you." He pulled up the collar and rubbed her hands. "I need to get you back to the cabin."

The aroma of pine and snow were everywhere, but the mustiness of his coat surprised her.

Since he wore it doing all his chores, she expected the fabric to smell more like sweat. But there was no essence of him. If anything, the scent reminded her of an article of clothing that had hung in a closet for a very long time.

He picked up the lantern and took her hand. "I haven't been on this side of the property in ..." He paused. "Just stay close to me."

He led the way through the trees, holding his lantern to guide them.

She could barely see beyond the dim light.

Courtney anxiously searched the trees. "What was that thing I saw back there? I swear it was a giant cat."

"Could have been a cougar or bobcat." He remained calm, his focus on the terrain ahead. "They've been seen around here."

"And what about that hill?" She tugged his coat closer, grateful for the warmth. "Someone had cleared around the base and at the top."

He didn't turn back to her as he forged ahead. "I don't know of any hill around here."

She wanted to interrogate him. He must know every inch of

his property. Once she was in front of a warm fire inside the shelter of her cabin, she would press him for more information.

The lantern's light shone on a small path, carved between the trees. Heavy rocks lined the slim trail, and the snow didn't appear as heavy.

Courtney wanted to jump for joy. It was the first sign of civilization she'd seen in hours. "We must be getting close to the cabins."

Peter didn't say anything. He kept his shoulders and head lowered. The change in him bothered her. She was about to ask him what was wrong when the thick line of trees on either side of the path thinned.

The trail dipped as they came to an embankment. Then rays from the stars popped out, reflecting off something before them.

The river.

They had reached the river and the sight confounded Courtney. She hadn't been that far from it. The density of the woods had hidden the waterway when she stood on the rise. She must have been walking in circles for hours. But she had paid attention, tried to find landmarks, and still she had no clue of how to retrace her steps.

There were no footprints.

Peter led her along the shoreline. The frozen river helped to ease the nightmare of being chased by a diabolical creature.

Then something rose from the frozen river. Lit by the night sky, the gentle arch and rough beams of the bridge materialized.

Her grip on his hand tightened. "I don't understand how I got so turned around."

Peter hesitated before he stepped onto the bridge. "It's easy to do. These woods are not kind."

She grabbed the railing, thrilled to be close to the cabin. She caressed the smooth wood, but then her fingers encountered something out of place.

The rough patch sat lower than the railing, but when her fingers touched the familiar figure of a letter, she halted.

Courtney pulled at Peter's hand holding the lantern. She raised the candle over the spot on the railing.

She gasped when she spotted Evelyn's beautifully carved name gleaming in the light.

Somehow, she had ended up on the other side of the river. She remembered what Mrs. Finn told her about Peter's fear of crossing the bridge. What he must have overcome to search for her wiped away the last pangs of trauma from her harrowing experience.

"You came across the bridge?" She took in the serene setting and grew quiet, numbed by the realization of what he had done. "You said you hadn't gone to the other side of the river since … but you did now. I can't believe you did for me."

"You make it sound like you're not worth it."

The dim lamplight hid his face, but the tenderness in his voice chased away the last of her distress.

She faced the water, ashamed. "I'm not. All my life I've doubted myself. I was never pretty enough or smart enough. I blamed my dad, my past for holding me back. Every man I wanted was wrong. I thought you were repeating that history. Then when you just left me that day, I was convinced I would be doomed to a life without love." She motioned to the bridge. "But then you do something like this, overcome the horror of your past for me, and I'm …" She couldn't find the words.

"I couldn't leave you out there to die," Peter said, lowering the lamp. "I stood on this bridge and thought of you alone and scared, and you were all that mattered."

She stepped closer, her hope for something more with Peter sent tingles to her cold toes. "No one has ever done anything like that for me before."

"No, I am not the first, and I won't be the last." He cupped her cheek, bringing his lips closer. "You're worth every trial, every tear, because you are the world to those who love you. You reminded me we are the sum of the love we hold in our hearts. When we forget that, we lose sight of everything that makes us worthwhile."

Tears welled in her eyes. The icy walls she'd spent years building to protect her fragile heart cracked. The hurt she'd nursed retreated and an interest in something more with someone special blossomed.

"It's been a very long time since anyone has made … No, let me rephrase that, since I have let anyone make me feel special."

His thumb grazed her cheek. "You will always be special to me."

She waited, hoping for a kiss, expecting that perfect moment to end in a happily ever after, but Peter removed his hand and stood back.

"Time to get you home."

Courtney floundered between disappointment and elation. She replayed every word he'd spoken, injecting her varied interpretations into his meaning.

So where do we stand?

Preoccupied with wondering about his feelings, and trying to make sense of hers, Courtney didn't pay much attention as they maneuvered the path back to the cabin. The occasional glint of the candlelight on a few stones she recognized, or a familiar clump of trees would distract her, but then Peter's words would spin in her head like an out-of-control washing machine.

The reassuring glow of lights brought a smile to her lips. The tension in her neck and shoulders eased when she saw the outline of her cabin. The aroma of burning wood quickened her aching feet. Images of the fireplace and packed refrigerator had her almost breaking into a run the last few yards.

Twinkling lights of blue, red, green, and white shone through the window that looked out from the dining area. The strange display awakened a funny sense of unease in her gut.

She stopped and stared, wondering how the Christmas lights she destroyed could be working and hanging on her tree.

Peter encouraged her toward the cabin with a nudge. Courtney took the last few steps no longer fretting about what Peter had said, but more concerned with what he had done.

He climbed the back steps and pushed the door open.

The warmth embraced her, bringing needles to her numb cheeks.

The kitchen smelled of warmed butter and coffee. She took in the aroma as Peter came up behind her.

"I put the coffee on before I went searching for you." He eased his coat from around her shoulders. "You need to get warmed up by the fire."

The lights in the dining area took her breath away.

Her hands trembled as she examined the Christmas tree decorated in silver balls and streams of glistening garland. Colorful circles of light dotted the walls and ceiling, adding to the joy filling her heart.

She couldn't remember the last time anything had touched her so profoundly. What the decorated evergreen represented—Peter's kindness toward her—made her feel very special.

"How did ...?" She didn't know where to begin. "There weren't any decorations left. I ripped them to shreds last night. Where did you find more?"

He put a blanket around her shoulders. "Why did you destroy my decorations?"

"I was mad. My mother told me something about my dad I didn't want to hear, and I lashed out. I'm sorry. I'll pay for—"

"Forget it." He admired the tree. "It's more important you have this tree for Christmas Eve. I would feel better knowing you had something to remind you of the hope that is still inside you."

She grinned. "My hope? In a Christmas tree?"

He went back to the counter and picked up his coat. "I told you about the children in olden times who would decorate their trees with ornaments that represented the hopes for their future. This tree is your hope for a shining future filled with love. You deserve that, Courtney, very much."

He shrugged his coat on and guided her to the living room, then moved to set a log on the fire.

How could she look at a Christmas tree again without

thinking of Peter? Perhaps the shining future he mentioned would be with him. The notion melted her concerns about letting another man into her life. She and love had a shaky relationship, but the warmth Peter created dissolved her misgivings. The time had come to take down the walls around her heart.

The moment she sank into the sofa cushions, pins and needles rose in her hands. She could barely close her fist without wincing. Once she kicked off her wet shoes, she put her numb toes closer to the fire.

Peter handed her a cup of coffee, and she took a sip and smiled.

"Thank you. I don't think I will ever be able to get up again." She leaned back. "I feel like I've been hit by a truck." She longed to sleep for days, but her mind would not let her.

Watching him stoke the fire, Courtney said, "There are still things I don't understand."

"Such as?"

"Why did you come here today?" She pulled the blanket tighter around her shoulders. "You haven't been here for two days."

He came up to the sofa. "I had a feeling you needed me, and I was right. When I found the door open, and you didn't return soon, I went in search of you." He sat next to her. "You're lucky I found you when I did. Otherwise, you would have ended up …" His voice trailed away.

"Like you?" she added. "I know what happened to you at the river. Mrs. Finn told me."

He stiffened at the mention of the older woman. "Well, I won't have to deal with her for much longer."

Alarm snaked through her and she set the coffee down. "What are you talking about?"

Peter took her hand, rubbing it to get her warm. "I have to leave soon, but thank you for helping me make this decision. Without you, I might have stayed here and continued to …"

She retracted her hand and all the warm feelings he'd created in her disintegrated. "Leave? You mean leave the lodge, or me?"

He tipped his head, a weak smile on his lips. "I'm sure there will be a part of me that remains with you for a very long time to come. But I must go. I've spent too much time here hiding from the truth. I'm not this man anymore." He waved his hand down his brown pants and high boots. "I was never ready to accept what I'd become until I met you. You showed me that embracing what is will always be better than holding on to what can never be."

Courtney rubbed her temples, confused. "I don't understand. Where are you going? How can you walk away from your business, your family? Back in the woods, you told me—"

He took her hand. "I'm not sure I can ever find a way to make you understand, but I want you to promise me something. Don't shut out the next person who wants to get to know you. Give him a chance."

Courtney stood, a wave of dizziness overtook her, and she teetered. "What are you talking about?"

Peter helped her back to the sofa. "A man will greet you in the morning. I want you to be kind to him, listen to him. Give him a chance."

The cold flush spread through her. "What man? I don't understand. Don't you want me? I thought we were …"

He gripped both her hands, squeezing them tight. "There's someone you need to let in because he is like you. You have so much in common and deserve happiness."

A faint voice from a memory drifted through her tattered mind. There were many emotions, many frenzied images, clouding her judgment, but Lynn's voice came to the forefront of her thoughts.

"How did you know?" She stared at their intertwined hands, uncertainty coiling in her chest. "Lynn said the same thing to me."

The lines around his eyes cut deeper into his skin. "Who is Lynn?"

"The woman who saved me the night I got locked out of the cabin. She showed up with a lantern just like yours—lit by a single candle. She told me I should give you a chance. She said you were a good man and that we have a lot in common."

Peter let her go and rocked back on the sofa.

His sudden distance brought the knot in her chest to her throat.

"Are you all right?"

"What did she look like?"

"Blonde, pretty, with the cutest dimples in her cheeks. She was out in the woods looking at the stars and said her cabin wasn't too far from mine."

Peter stood and combed his hand through his hair. "She was here?"

The quivering muscles in his clenched jaw distressed her. "Peter, what's going on?"

"I have to go to the bridge. I have to find her."

In two long strides, Peter was at the door. He yanked it open. The cold breeze that blew through the living room awakened horrible memories of the terrifying woods.

"What? Why?" she asked, getting to her feet.

Peter didn't glance back as he barreled through the door.

His heavy footfalls across the porch echoed around the room.

Still wrapped in her blanket, Courtney went to the door and peered out into the night.

The brisk air went right through her, eliciting a chill, then she caught the outline of Peter's silhouette. His long black coat flapped in the slight breeze before he disappeared into the shadows surrounding the trees.

The cold forgotten, she went onto the porch and stared into the darkness.

"Why are you going to the bridge?" she whispered.

He didn't return to explain. There was only the faint whisper of wind.

A sinister foreboding clung to her, shrinking the world around her and chasing away the frigid night. Courtney dreaded the prospect of venturing back into the woods, but she had to make sense of his irrational behavior. She had to know how Peter could say the things he did and then walk away. If she didn't go after him, Courtney would regret it for the rest of her life.

She dashed back inside and shrugged off the blanket. At the back door, she grabbed her thick coat and slipped on her boots. She returned to the living room and picked up one of the lanterns by the door.

Courtney stepped onto the porch. The white halo from the

lantern illuminated the clearing around the cabin, but there was no sign of Peter and no footprints in the snow.

Bile burned the back of her throat, encouraging her to go back inside, but if Courtney walked away, she might forfeit her chance to discover what was going on with Peter.

Who did he have to find?

Chapter Twenty-One

The endless black in the woods closed around Courtney when she stepped onto the path between the trees. She tensed—the images of the catlike creature still fresh in her mind. She sucked in a calming breath, held it, and listened. No growling sounds, no frenzied footfalls of someone running, or even the disturbed cries of a man getting eaten, echoed through the night. Encouraged, she pressed on down the path.

The lamp made the trek easier by shedding light on every stone and dip, but it also illuminated dozens of eyes staring back at her from behind trees. The scary orbs weren't orange, and appeared less threatening, but the way they followed her didn't help her frayed nerves.

Courtney stuck to the path and, thanks to the lantern, was able to pick out several landmarks from her walk with Peter a few days ago—the funny shaped rock with odd wings jutting from its center, and a crooked tree bent over to the side.

Resilience replaced her fear. Insulated from the cold, and her courage bourgeoning with every step, she concentrated on finding Peter.

The full rising moon broke from behind a patch of clouds. An unworldly glow brushed aside the darkness and displaced the night. She'd never seen the woods highlighted in such a breathtaking display. The magic of Christmas Eve had changed the landscape from gloomy to hauntingly serene.

The ground sloped, the trees thinned, and rocks covered the landscape. Courtney quickly arrived at the frozen river's edge and raised her lantern, searching for the bridge.

Thanks to the moonlight, the structure wasn't hard to find. Courtney sighed when she found a lone figure on the boards, wearing a long coat and peering across to the opposite shore. Peter's features remained hidden by the shadows.

"Peter!"

She ran as fast as she could over the craggy shore toward the bridge. She kept her lantern lifted, constantly checking to make sure he didn't move.

At the step to the bridge, she slowed. Courtney walked calmly toward him, approaching like she would a skittish horse.

He frantically scoured the opposite shore with his mouth set in a grim line and edginess wrinkling his brow.

Curiosity burned as she reached his side. With a hesitant hand, she went to gently tug at his elbow. Her hand didn't connect with the wool of his coat, but instead passed right through the fabric. Thinking it a result of her fatigue, she went to touch him again, but her hand sank through the essence of him until it connected with the railing on the bridge.

Courtney gasped, blood roaring through her veins. Shock left her speechless. She tucked her hand against her chest and took a step backward.

Peter turned to her, smiling and happier than she had ever seen. An odd light, golden and glimmering, came from him. A pulsating halo covering the surface of his skin and clothes, radiating an energy that made her hair stand on end.

Not sure what to make of any of it, Courtney lifted her lantern, hoping in some silly way the added light could explain the strange phenomenon. Instead, her stomach clenched, and the acidic taste of fright filled her mouth.

"Peter? What's going on? Why do you look—"

He held out his arms, and the glow emanating from him expanded, circling him in a large ball. He reminded her of The Vitruvian Man, encased in a light that illuminated the frozen river and surrounding land. The change didn't hurt her eyes or make her want to run back to the cabin. The energy coming from him soothed and mesmerized, quieting the churn of her dread.

"This is me, Courtney. The real me."

She felt trapped in a dream. The bridge and river swayed. The trees caught in the light seemed to expand and contract. Courtney shook her head, willing her senses back.

"I don't understand what's happening."

He stepped closer. "When you first came outside and saw me chopping wood, you weren't afraid. You came up to me, speaking to me as if I were a man. You didn't see me for what I am—a spirit."

"Spirit?" Courtney set her lantern down and marched up to him. "Peter, I don't know what is going on here. Maybe you need help, but you're not a ghost. You're as real—"

A shimmering behind him dried up her words. It was

228

surrounded by the same golden essence as him, illuminating the opposite side of the bridge with its powerful light. The flowing figure glided out to the side, allowing Courtney a better look.

A woman in a gown of white silk floated alongside Peter. The tapered sleeves of her dress ended in cuffs of delicate white lace. A collar ran from her neck to the scoop of her bustline. Her waist, cinched into a tight brocade bodice of silver thread, glistened with an array of pearls and beads. Embroidery trimming the hem helped hide her feet beneath yards of layered fabric.

"Hello, Courtney."

Her voice was as airy as the first time they met. Her golden hair flowed behind her, secured with a pearl barrette, and her smile accentuated the dimples in her pink cheeks.

"Lynn?" Her jaw slipped open. "What are you doing here?"

"Her name is Evelyn," Peter said in a hushed tone. "Lynn was the nickname I gave her."

Courtney inched closer, no longer concerned about the weird light. "Evelyn? You're Evelyn? But how? Shouldn't she be with your brother, Lawrence? And what about that dress? It's got to be—"

"My wedding dress," Evelyn cut in. "I was buried in it not long after I married Lawrence. I lost my will to live when Peter died and have been waiting for him to return to me ever since."

A pressure squeezed Courtney's chest and she fought to get in a breath. Her knees wobbled and she bent over to grab them.

This can't be happening.

Peter stepped toward her. "Because of your help, I felt alive for the first time since the day I drowned at this bridge."

Courtney bolted upright and shook her head. She wanted to run but was too terrified to move. "No. I touched you. I could feel you. I ..."

"Your belief in me made me real." Peter took Evelyn's hand. "And it's because of you I was able to break the bonds holding me to this place. You helped me overcome my fear and go beyond the bridge."

Courtney glanced down at the boards beneath her feet. "The bridge. You couldn't cross it before, but you did when you rescued me."

Evelyn curled her hand around Peter's arm. "I've been waiting for him to let go. I knew the moment I saw you that you would help free him."

Courtney leaned against the railing, lightheaded and queasy. "I fell asleep on the sofa. That's it. You can't be real."

"Spirits are just as real as you. We just learned to be patient for our happily ever after." Evelyn gazed into Peter's happy face. "Our families and sense of duty kept us apart in life, but there are no more earthly binds to separate us. You have taken care of that."

"I still don't understand," Courtney whispered.

Peter moved away from Evelyn and came up to Courtney. "I was told if I ventured beyond the bounds of the river, my soul would cease to exist, and I would never be with Evelyn. But I had to take that chance, make that sacrifice, to save you. Instead of destroying me, it saved me. I want to thank you for that."

Shock mixed with the heaviness in her heart, and then something he said resonated. "Who told you that?"

Evelyn came forward, the skirts of her dress swaying beneath her. "It's time to go."

"Go? Go where?" Courtney's throat tightened. "Can't you stay and tell me more?"

Peter touched her cheek, but all she felt was a breath of wind tickling her skin.

"I wish I could, but it's Christmas Day—a time for new beginnings for both of us." He lowered his hand. "Promise me you will embrace the man who comes to greet you when the sun rises. He deserves a chance."

A rush of uncertainty gripped her. "What man?"

Peter only smiled and then returned to Evelyn's side. The love shining in his eyes silenced her questions.

Their happiness reminded her of how empty her life would be without him. Ghost or not, he had filled a hole left by many others. He'd also given her the story her heart wanted to write. There was still so much she wanted to know.

Peter and Evelyn's joined bodies ignited a brilliant white light. It exploded around them, expanding the circle immersing them, and almost blinded Courtney. She shielded her eyes, but no heat followed, only a surge of joy and love. She reveled in the high of the emotions filling her heart. She had never felt so complete.

Then the blazing light dimmed. In increments, the intensity lessened, and the circle around the couple grew smaller. The orb shrank, slowly dimming, until all that was left was the faint outline of their joined figures. The dark closed in, encroaching on the circle and replacing the love they generated with a chilly breeze.

She wiped away her tears. "Thank you, for everything."

The glow that had defined them shrank to the size of a tennis ball, which floated above the bridge, round and unwavering. The faint light dimmed and closed in on itself, surrendering inch by inch to the night.

Before the last speck disappeared, the faintest cackle carried through the air. The horrid, hateful sound brought back the cold to Courtney's bones.

She picked up her lantern and searched the land on either side of the bridge for the sound, but no one was there. Perhaps it was the wind or the call of an owl.

Courtney hugged her lantern, overcome by the roller coaster of emotions the last few days had created. She thought back on Peter's clothes, his weird comings and goings, and how he was never around when Mrs. Finn was at the cabin. It all added up, but she had to admit, Peter being a spirit hadn't been on her list of reasons behind his suspicious behavior.

She remembered Peter's warning about the quirks of the cabin.

He wasn't kidding.

The depth and breadth of her wounds were not what they once were. It had taken a ghost to show her the value of life and love. But Peter had returned to Evelyn, and Courtney felt the progress she'd made would be lost without him.

To know the couple had found happiness together did ease her sorrow. The happy ending robbed from them in life, they received in death.

Self-doubt came back like a blazing comet, ripping her heart in two. She hadn't been the woman for him either.

Alone on the bridge, surrounded by darkness and woods, Courtney found it ironic that she grieved for a man who had died long ago.

You always did make the worst choices in men.

Chapter Twenty-Two

*C*ourtney wallowed in her sadness. Though, knowing what waited for everyone after their last breath gave her some comfort. Still, she had a long life to get through before she could find peace, and who would be waiting for her on the other side?

Maybe it's time to get a dog.

Fingers of lights appeared on the boards around her. They landed on her boot and traveled up her coat. She reached for the yellow beams, questioning where they came from.

She glanced up. The night had passed, and the sun's rays stretched over the bridge and frozen river. The light caressed the tops of the trees, arousing a frenzy of birdsong.

Courtney raised her head to the sun, relishing the warmth. The pure white of the snow covering the land reflected the brightness of the sunrise. The crisp aroma of pine, the shimmer of the frozen river, even the motion of the fish swimming below invigorated her tired body.

A new day—Christmas Day—and unlike every other sunrise, this one became special because she appreciated it more than the rest.

She was alive in a world of beautiful things. Perhaps the time had come to stop languishing on what she didn't have and cherish what she did. From this moment on, Courtney would relish every minute. All the negativity she'd held on to suddenly became pointless.

She stayed on the bridge, watching the sunrise.

Then heavy footfalls echoed across the bridge, tearing her attention away from the sky.

"Courtney?"

The voice was male, deep, slightly musical, and brought a confused frown to her face.

When she turned around, a man in jeans and a thick leather jacket stood behind her. The wind tossed his blond hair as he stared at her, a deep line cutting across his brow.

"Are you all right?"

"Peter? You're back?" Her heart sped up, banging against her chest. He had returned to her.

Peter came up to her, inspecting her with his steely blue gaze. "Are you all right? What are you doing out here?"

She touched his leather jacket and examined his blue jeans. "Your clothes. They're different."

He opened his jacket and stared at his thick boots. "This is what I always wear around the lodge."

Ice, colder than any she'd encountered in the mountains, formed in her veins.

"You look just like …" Her voice stilled.

He squinted at her, and a crease formed on his smooth brow. "Who do I look like?"

Her brain stuttered, coming to terms with the impossible. The world around her slowed as her thoughts raced to catch up.

"How long have you been out here?" Peter stepped closer, pulling her jacket around her. "I need to get you warm before hypothermia sets in."

She studied his eyes and then saw it—the color was more intense, more iridescent than before. The dullness wasn't there. This man was vibrant and alive.

"It's not you, is it?"

"I'm me, Courtney. The same man I was the first day you met me at the lodge."

The urgency with which he escorted her off the bridge didn't feel the same as when she had been with the other Peter. This man was different, but the strength in his arms brought comfort, and the warmth of him calmed her.

Even the smell of him as he put his arm around her, musky and seductive, was not like her Peter.

She said nothing as he guided her along the path that led to her cabin. There were two Peters—one a ghost and one a living man. How had that happened?

Her mind numb with overthinking, she climbed the steps, worn out from the long night.

"I came by and found you gone. I got worried." Peter followed her. "After you called the other day, I've been wanting to check on you, but I didn't want to impose or know how you'd feel about that."

She stopped at the top of the steps and faced him. "It was you I called, wasn't it? I thought …" She put her hand to her head. "I'm not sure what I thought."

Peter rushed ahead and opened the door. "Let me get the fire going to warm you up."

She stopped at the threshold to the cabin and peered inside. The living room was the same, and her computer remained on the sofa where she'd left it. Courtney thought of her story, and how she should change the ending and infuse some hope into her tale.

Peter grabbed the poker and jabbed at the black log atop the flames. It crumpled into large red embers.

She came inside and went to the fire. The heat took away her fogginess. She didn't realize how cold she was until painful tingles hijacked the sensation in her fingers.

Courtney stared into the flames, aware of Peter's gaze on her. He was so much like her Peter; she was almost afraid to look at him in case he dematerialized.

Peter dropped another log onto the grate. The crackling of the wood filled the void between them.

"I was glad to see you put up your tree," he said, sticking close to her. "Now you'll keep the old Yule Cat away."

The reference to the cat swept aside the cobwebs and she raised her head. "You've heard of the Yule Cat, too?"

He nodded to the beautiful woman carved into the front door that stood ajar. "I told you, my family came from Austria and brought a lot of their superstitions with them. My grandmother believed the Yule Cat came to those who didn't decorate their tree."

Perchta's liquid eyes drew Courtney in. She stared at the woman's face, still trying to find an explanation for the snarl she'd seen. Courtney couldn't explain the uneasy feeling in her depths, but she swore the woman carved in the front door had something to do with the strange events of the past few days.

She pointed at the door, the apprehensive flutter inside her growing. "Peter, who carved this?"

He came alongside her and tipped his head as he inspected the carving. "No one knows for sure, but I've always suspected it was the man who built this cabin."

The icy grip of dread returned to her belly. "Who was that?"

Peter turned to the cabin walls. "I'll show you."

He went to a far corner where there hung a single, lonely picture. He pointed at the solitary figure caught in the faded photo. "This is him."

Courtney slowly approached a picture she hadn't noticed before.

The man in the grainy photo stood at the base of the bridge over the river. He had one hand placed firmly on the rail as he looked into the camera. His long black coat hung from his tall frame, and his high black riding boots were dull. He didn't smile and seemed a little sad. She recognized the comma of hair across his forehead, the cut of his square jaw, and the pale light in his eyes.

"His name was Peter Morris, too." Peter's voice carried a hint of pride. "He was my great, great uncle who I was named after. There is always a Lawrence and a Peter in our family. It's tradition."

She touched the glass covering the picture and traced his face with her finger. "What happened to him?"

Peter walked back to the fire. "He drowned at the bridge where I found you. Some say because of a broken heart. I suspect he's the reason nothing works in this cabin. I've had numerous guests mention seeing a man in a long black coat and riding boots in the area." He bashfully lowered his head. "That's why I didn't feel comfortable renting this cabin to you alone. I was concerned you would be afraid. But when you said I was your last hope, I couldn't bring myself to tell you."

She boldly walked up to him. "What about Mrs. Finn? Why didn't she tell me about the ghost?"

Peter's eyes narrowed. "Who's Mrs. Finn?"

The warmth in the room dissipated, prickling her skin. "Mrs. Finn, the cook you sent to prepare meals."

He scratched his head. "Cook? Why would I stock the cabin and not tell you I was sending someone to cook? There is no one named Mrs. Finn working for the lodge."

Her chest constricted. Courtney fought the desire to lean over and grab her knees.

She was a ghost, too?

He held her arm as worry darkened his features. "Are you okay? You look as white as a sheet."

Courtney reined in her nervous breakdown. She straightened and summoned her best stoic accountant's face—the one she used with difficulty.

"I'm fine. Just tired and ..." She stopped and regrouped, hunting for an explanation. "I guess spending time alone in a cabin isn't all it's cracked up to be."

He motioned to her computer. "I hope you got some work done."

She offered him a slight smile. "I actually got a lot accomplished while I was here. More than I anticipated."

"Did you get your book finished?"

Courtney folded her arms, empowered by the path she was about to take. "No, I didn't. I found something else to write about. A story I believe in."

"I'm glad. You didn't seem too enthused about your other book. It would be a shame to waste your time on something that doesn't make you happy." Peter rubbed his hands together. "I hope after all your hard work, you're ready for a break."

A flutter of uncertainty danced in her belly. "A break?"

"I invited you to Christmas dinner at the lodge, remember?" A playful grin stretched across his lips. "It's the reason I'm here. I came to get you."

The dinner on Christmas Day. She had forgotten all about agreeing to go. After the long night on the bridge and her revelations, the idea of being surrounded by a bunch of strangers at a dinner table felt anticlimactic.

"Ah." She rubbed her arms, bristling with guilt. "I should get back to—"

"Promise me you will embrace the man who will greet you in the morning."

Peter's voice rang in her ears. He sounded loud enough to be right by her side, but he wasn't. There was no ghost in the room—no hint of his energy, nothing.

His memory melted her excuses, and her desire to be alone faded. As the ghost had said, the Peter standing before her deserved a chance.

"I would love to join you. Just let me get ready.

The beaming smile he gave sent a tingle to her toes. He

nervously combed his hand through his hair while a slight blush colored his cheeks. "Ah, great. I wasn't sure you would come. After that day we met, I didn't think you liked me too much."

Courtney took his hand and squeezed it. "I like you very much. I just needed to work some things out. And I have. I'm sorry I was so distant."

He inched closer, an alluring gleam in his eyes. "Can I get that in writing?"

She giggled. "I can arrange that."

Peter cupped her cheeks and gently pressed a lingering kiss to her forehead. Courtney felt an immediate warmth accompanied by butterflies in her stomach.

"I'm glad. I have a feeling we have a lot in common."

"Yeah," she whispered. "I have the same feeling."

The morning sun shone down on drifts of snow around the cabin, sending up a bright glare. Peter and Courtney exited the cabin, holding hands and laughing with each other. They climbed down the porch steps, appearing happy.

Peter helped her into his Jeep, parked not far from the porch steps. He stepped around to the driver's side door when something on the porch brought him to a halt.

He paused and scowled into the shadows, peering at the cabin door. After a few seconds, he shook his head and went to the other side of his vehicle.

The roar of the engine carried across the clearing. The big tires on the Jeep chomped the snowy path as it headed down the mountain toward the lodge.

The crunch of the tires soon dwindled, and peace returned to the clearing.

Then the wind kicked up, sending swaths of snow across the rustic porch.

The door to the cabin vibrated, shaking on its hinges. The wood swelled and contracted as if fighting for breath while an eerie creaking carried across the clearing. The face carved there swayed and rolled. A form pushed out, attempting to break free of its restraints. The woman's features stretched outward, bulging from the door like someone pressing through a balloon.

A woman's pale, tapered hand reached out as if checking the air. She wiggled her fingers, displaying long black fingernails. The door bloated, and an arm covered with blue sleeves followed. A shoulder eased out, and then the hourglass-shaped torso. She stepped from the door, and her bare feet touched the porch planks. Her long black hair slipped over her shoulder as she raised her head. Beautiful, with haunting blue eyes, a slender nose, and well-carved cheekbones, she scanned the clearing around the home. The silky fabric of her dress billowed, caught up in the gentle breeze.

She took a few steps on the porch while the door behind her shrank back to fit the frame. The carving of Perchta was gone, and only a few dark swirls of the wood remained.

The woman's gaze closed in on the path taken by Peter's Jeep. A snarl curled her full red lips, showing off her yellow teeth.

Wrinkles popped up on her face, becoming more pronounced

242

and spreading lines across her brow and around her mouth. Her skin sagged around her jawline and turned sallow. Then her long hair danced around her face, rising upward and twisting like coils of rope. The black color instantly changed, taking on a fiery red hue. Her sleek figure rounded, and the fabric of her dress changed from silky to a coarser cotton weave. Her bright red hair settled into a neat pile atop her head, and her long dress stretched, turning into a loose-fitting garment. On her bare feet, pointy black leather shoes appeared.

The alluring woman who had first walked out of the door no longer existed. Mrs. Finn stood in her place. The only feature they seemed to share was the same cruel snarl and ugly teeth.

Mrs. Finn walked toward the railing and snapped her fingers.

The wind swirling around the cabin instantly died. Snowflakes lifted by the breeze fell to the ground. Birds went silent, and animals frolicking in the trees became petrified. An unearthly hush settled over the land.

Mrs. Finn's furious gaze scanned the clearing. The creases around her small mouth and across her creamy brow deepened as she glared ahead.

She put her hands on her hips and sighed, the frustrated sound echoed across the clearing.

"Another soul lost." She stomped her foot on the floorboard. "I was so close with that girl. Might be some time before I can find another broken spirit."

Mrs. Finn scanned the clearing around the house and frowned.

"Living out here makes it hard to accomplish anything. Time

I move to the city. Should be lots of broken hearts like that silly girl, Courtney. Imagine all that I could collect there."

A rumble rolled across the woods.

A few squirrels in front of the cabin ran for shelter. The birds went silent, and a flock hurriedly took flight. They lifted from the trees around the house, their dark wings appearing as black dots across the blue sky.

The wind returned, cutting across the porch and billowing her dress. The snow on the porch got sucked into the wind. The flakes swirled around her and thickened until Mrs. Finn became caught in a snow-devil.

More snow from the steps, and even some from alongside the house, got swept into the vortex. Mrs. Finn soon became lost behind a spinning wall of white.

The whirling cyclone quickly slowed and broke apart. The snow captured in its rotation trickled back to the ground, leaving odd-shaped drifts along the edges of the porch and steps.

When the last of the wind died, Mrs. Finn had disappeared. What stood in her spot was the black cat. With gray ruff around its neck and unnatural orange eyes, the queen glared into the woods while the thump of her tail resonated across the porch.

She carefully stepped over the snow and then strutted across the floorboards.

The fluffy creature trotted down the steps and casually sauntered toward the trees.

Right before the cat reached the base of a sturdy pine, she glanced back at the cabin door.

The carving of the beautiful Perchta that had once adorned

the door never returned. Only dark swirls in the wood shone beneath the morning sun.

"Time to find a new home," the cat said in Mrs. Finn's craggy voice.

Its unearthly eyes shrank to two glowing slits, radiating with contempt. Then the mysterious feline strutted into the shadows and vanished into thin air.

Epilogue

One Year Later

*S*trains of a Christmas carol drifted over Courtney as she scribbled her signature inside a book. Before her, a woman with silver hair anxiously fidgeted while waiting for her autograph. When Courtney handed over the novel, the diamond ring on her left hand caught in the twinkling tea lights strewn across the store's bookcases.

"I hope you like it," Courtney said to the woman.

The fan clutched the book to her chest. "Like it? I love it. I've already read it twice on my Kindle. The way Peter meets Evelyn on the bridge he built for her. How they run away together, and he gives up his family fortune ..." She wiped a tear from her eye. "I cried like a baby. How did you ever come up with such an unforgettable tale?"

A squeeze on Courtney's shoulder made her glance up.

Peter's lively blue eyes greeted her, taking her breath away. All thoughts of past heartbreaks had left her long ago. The only worries plaguing her now were whether she'd picked the right china for their new condo and if her wedding dress would be ready come the big day.

Courtney smiled at Peter, and then faced her reader.

"I got the idea when I spent some time alone in the woods with a special friend."

Peter kissed her cheek and murmured, "You're talking about me, right?"

His voice was still musical, but part of her missed the spirit who had carried his sadness like a mantle. Knowing that ghostly Peter was with his Evelyn gave her some consolation, but Courtney still longed for a rematch on the river. Maybe one day, they would meet and play hockey again.

She squeezed Peter's hand. "Who else would I be talking about?"

Content with her newly signed novel, the older woman walked away, wearing a beaming smile.

Peter sat on the edge of the table and selected a book from the stack next to Courtney. He eyed the blue cover with an ethereal couple locked in a tender embrace.

"I still can't believe you came up with a bestselling novel while staying in my creepy cabin."

Courtney stood and stretched her back. "It wasn't that creepy."

Peter put the book aside. "But you wouldn't want to go there for our honeymoon, right?"

She put her arms around him. "And give up the beach at Waikiki. Are you mad?"

He held her close. "No, I suppose surf is better than snow."

Peter touched his lips to hers, and the spark he aroused in her burned. She gently kissed him back, hungry for more, but also mindful of the customers taking in their display.

She pulled back and brushed away a lock of blond hair that had fallen into his eyes.

"I'm starving." He let her go. "Where can we eat around here?"

Courtney giggled and held his hand. "In downtown Nashville, there are a ton of places. What do you feel like?"

He put his arm around her. "Nashville hot chicken. How does that sound?"

She cringed as the aroma of Mrs. Finn's burnt chicken came back to her.

"How about pizza? I know a great place around the corner."

Peter motioned to the bookstore entrance. "Lead the way."

Courtney patted his chest. "Let me just tell the manager we are leaving and thank them for having me."

Peter nodded. "I understand. I'll wait here why you talk book business."

She gave him one last smile, and then the image of the last time she'd seen her ghost warmed her heart.

I guess we both got our second chance, after all.

Snowflakes gathered on the corners of the bookstore display window situated along the busy downtown street. Holiday shoppers, their arms filled with packages, rushed past the arrangement of books that promised love and happy endings.

In the corner of the showcase, curled on top of the swath of red cloth, a large black cat napped next to Courtney's book.

The queen ignored the patrons in the store, but then a couple exited, and their joyous laughter roused her.

When she stretched out her front paws, yawning with satisfaction, the black furry beast opened her macabre orange eyes.

Peter and Courtney walked past the window, and the feline hissed at them. The couple appeared oblivious to the angry mouser intently watching as they strolled away.

The animal daintily stepped around the books, but before departing, took a swipe at Courtney's novel.

The tome toppled just as the cat leaped to the floor and headed toward the entrance.

Once outside, the honorary creature shook its thick coat and scanned the street. And before she moved away, a woman's grisly laugh skirted along the sidewalk before ascending into the darkening sky. Then the queen trotted into the bustling street, but before any car could get close, she dashed across the road and disappeared into a corner lot filled with a selection of fir trees waiting to find a home for Christmas.

About the Author

Alexandrea Weis, RN-CS, PhD, is a multi-award-winning author, screenwriter, advanced practice registered nurse, and historian who was born and raised in the French Quarter of New Orleans. Having grown up in the motion picture industry as the daughter of a director, she learned to tell stories from a different perspective. Infusing the rich tapestry of her hometown into her novels, she believes that creating vivid characters makes a story moving and memorable.

Weis writes romance, mystery, suspense, thrillers, horror, paranormal, and young adult fiction and has sold approximately one million books. She lives with her husband and pets in New Orleans where she is a permitted/certified wildlife rehabber with the Louisiana Wildlife and Fisheries and rescues orphaned and injured animals.

She is a member of both the International Thriller Writers Association and the Horror Writers Association.

www.AlexandreaWeis.com